"We're behaving like the triplets are ours."

Kurt leaned close enough to kiss her—and didn't. "They will be soon."

"We don't even know for sure that they are *yours*."

His eyes roamed her face with disturbing intensity, lingering on her lips for a heart-stopping moment before returning to her eyes. "I have to believe they were left with me for a reason."

Paige studied him, wanting to understand Kurt the way he needed to be understood. "Because they needed a daddy."

"Because they were meant to bring me to you."

Dear Reader,

The McCabes of Texas are back! Greta and Shane McCabe, from *A Cowboy's Woman* (AR 797), have produced three sons and one daughter.

Hank McCabe is a military helicopter pilot who has returned to civilian life, intending to start his own cattle operation the old-fashioned way, with savings and hard work. The only person standing in his way is Ally Garrett, the owner of the ranch he wants.

Emily McCabe owns the Daybreak Café in Laramie. Tired of her family's interference in her love life, she hooks up with the worst catch possible, Dylan Reeves, a horse wrangler/whisperer who has sworn he will never be tamed by any woman.

Cattle breeder Jeb McCabe is convinced marriage and children aren't for him. Until he makes a bet and finds himself "playing house" with Cady Keiler and her rambunctious nephews.

Horse rancher Holden McCabe has clandestinely promised to look after widow Libby Lowell. And that means getting her to forget the emotional secret they are both keeping.

And last but not least—kicking off Texas Legacies: The McCabes is the story of veterinarian Kurt McCabe and his longtime rival. Pediatric surgeon Paige Chamberlain is the only daughter of Beau Chamberlain and Dani Lockhart Chamberlain, from *The Bride Said, "I Did?"* (AR 837). Kurt is the son of Annie and Travis McCabe, from *A Cowboy Kind of Daddy* (AR 801). Paige and Kurt have always driven each other crazy…until they find themselves temporarily parenting abandoned triplets.

Welcome back to Laramie, Texas, and the families who make it such a warm and wonderful place to visit.

Happy reading,

Cathy Gillen Thacker

Cathy Gillen Thacker

THE TRIPLETS'
FIRST THANKSGIVING

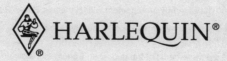

HARLEQUIN®

TORONTO • NEW YORK • LONDON
AMSTERDAM • PARIS • SYDNEY • HAMBURG
STOCKHOLM • ATHENS • TOKYO • MILAN • MADRID
PRAGUE • WARSAW • BUDAPEST • AUCKLAND

Recycling programs
for this product may
not exist in your area.

ISBN-13: 978-0-373-75329-1

THE TRIPLETS' FIRST THANKSGIVING

Copyright © 2010 by Cathy Gillen Thacker

Printed in U.S.A.

ABOUT THE AUTHOR

Cathy Gillen Thacker is married and a mother of three. She and her husband spent eighteen years in Texas and now reside in North Carolina. Her mysteries, romantic comedies and heartwarming family stories have made numerous appearances on bestseller lists, but her best reward, she says, is knowing one of her books made someone's day a little brighter. A popular Harlequin author for many years, she loves telling passionate stories with happy endings, and thinks nothing beats a good romance and a hot cup of tea! You can visit Cathy's Web site at www.cathygillenthacker.com for more information on her upcoming and previously published books, recipes and a list of her favorite things.

Books by Cathy Gillen Thacker

Chapter One

Kurt McCabe had been a burr under her saddle for as long as she could remember, but this was really the last straw!

Paige stared at the six-foot-five-inch Texan with tousled, dark brown hair and McCabe blue eyes. Thanks to her penchant for avoiding trouble—and their medical and veterinary educations, which had relocated them both for several years—she had managed to steer clear of her childhood nemesis for nearly a decade. If one discounted the huge family Thanksgiving gathering several Laramie, Texas, clans held jointly every year, that was! On that day, he managed to get under her skin, same as always....

Then another year would go by, and she'd forget all about him. Or at least try...knowing it would be months before she was likely to run into the handsome scoundrel again.

But now here he was back, living in their hometown, same as she. And much to her chagrin, Kurt McCabe was as sexy, masculine—and downright irritating—as ever.

At her continued silence, Kurt goaded her with "the

look" that never failed to send her blood pressure sky-rocketing. Paige turned back to Rowdy Whitcombe, another childhood friend. Determined to get a grip on her flaring temper, she enunciated clearly, "You cannot let McCabe jump line like this! You have to replace the plumbing in my house first!"

"I'm not jumping line," Kurt interjected, a smug smile dominating the rugged contours of his face. "You and I have both been waiting on the same shipment of pipe and fittings and it just got here today."

Paige glared at him, highly annoyed to have returned home from work to find the Rowdy Whitcombe Plumbing truck parked in front of Kurt McCabe's century-old Victorian instead of hers. Judging by the empty boxes on the front lawn, work had already begun on this project. "I signed my contract before you did, McCabe," she pointed out.

Kurt lifted a dark brow. "Actually, Paige, you signed yours on the *same day* I signed mine. I checked."

Know-it-all, she fumed. "It was still *before* yours—three hours before yours." Because had she known the two of them would be competing for Rowdy's time and skill, Paige would have gone elsewhere to get workable plumbing put in her home. Even as far as Fort Worth, if necessary! She swung around to their short, stocky friend. "Right, Rowdy?"

"Well, yes…" He blushed to the roots of his pale blond hair.

"Then…?" At five foot eleven, Paige towered over Rowdy.

The disconcerted plumber withdrew the red bandanna from his back pocket and rubbed it across his face. "Kurt wanted PVC pipe. You wanted copper. The PVC came off the delivery truck first. So, technically, even though *you* went under contract first, Paige, the materials for his job were *here* first."

She drew a long, calming breath. "So you decided to work on his house first." Her voice dripped with disdain.

Rowdy matched her eye roll with one of his own. "Give me a break, Paige. I owe Kurt for saving my horse."

She could hardly compete with that, so she fell back on the immutable facts. "This isn't personal, Rowdy. It's business."

"Actually, Paige," Kurt stated, with the authority all the implacable McCabe men seemed born with, "all business is personal...if it's done right."

She wished she could argue that, but she couldn't. "Don't call me by my first name," she snapped. She hated the way "Paige" sounded rolling off his lips, all falsely intimate and totally smart-aleck.

"You'd prefer sweetheart or darlin' or sugarplum...?"

Paige shook off the shivers prickling down her spine and sent him a withering glare. "Dr. Chamberlain would be fine."

He smiled condescendingly. "All right, Dr. Chamberlain, you can address *me* as Dr. McCabe."

"If you two are done with your, um, contest," Rowdy interrupted with a long-suffering grin, "I've got to get the rest of the PVC out of this truck."

Paige hadn't gotten to be one of the most prominent pediatric surgeons in the state of Texas by giving up, any more than Kurt had gotten to be a top-notch veterinarian by acquiescing. "Rowdy, I beg of you, please move the work on Kurt's home—"

"That's Dr. McCabe's home, to you," Kurt interrupted glibly.

Scoffing, Paige continued "—to the appropriate place in the line of those waiting for a complete plumbing overhaul." Sadly, her neighborhood was full of homes needing repair. It seemed all the fifty-year-old pipe had decided to rust through and disintegrate at once. Hence, any home that hadn't already been completely replumbed was in trouble, or about to be. Which was good for the Rowdy Whitcombe Plumbing Company. Not so good for everyone else, facing either monumental repairs or the risk of further burst pipes and resultant flooding.

Rowdy's jaw clenched. "No can do," he snapped back.

"But—"

The plumber held up a work-gloved hand and looked her square in the eye. "You're free to hire someone else if you want, Paige. I won't hold a grudge. But I'm working on Kurt's house first."

Paige knew further arguing would get her nowhere.

"I still promise to get you back into your home by Christmas," he said.

That was four and a half weeks away! "I wanted to be there by Thanksgiving," she reminded him flatly.

Rowdy continued collapsing the emptied cardboard boxes. "What's the big deal? Can't you just stay with your folks on their ranch?"

The big deal was this put a definite crimp in her secret plan to finally get a family of her very own. In order for everything to be perfect from the onset, she needed privacy—and plenty of sleep! But she wasn't about to confide in Rowdy—or heaven forbid, Kurt McCabe!— about that. Running water in her house or not, she was determined to carry out her mission in just eight days. She'd deal with the personal fallout from her actions later.

Paige shook her head. "No can do. My dad is overseeing the editing of the last movie he directed—and meeting with his producers about the next one—and my mom is putting the finishing touches on a new book of film reviews. Their guesthouse and every guest room is occupied." She sighed. "To make matters worse, all the hotel rooms in town are taken by the models involved in the catalog shoot for my aunt Jenna's new fashion line."

Once again, Kurt seemed intrigued, but not in a way Paige appreciated. Which was probably the point—to get under her skin, as usual.

"Still sleeping in an on-call room at the hospital then?" Rowdy asked.

Kurt turned his full attention to her once again. She ignored his laserlike gaze and the warm way it made her feel. She didn't want him imagining her curled up on one of the utilitarian bunk beds. Although he seemed to be doing exactly that...!

With a huff, she turned back to Rowdy. "It makes sense to sleep at the hospital, since I'm there all the time, anyway." A resentful edge entered her voice. "That doesn't mean it's a comfortable arrangement, when I have a large, beautiful home just blocks from the hospital waiting for me." Or it had been beautiful until her kitchen pipe had burst while she was at work, flooding the entire first floor.

Unsympathetic, Kurt shrugged. He challenged her with a lift of his chiseled chin. "I'm sure you could figure out a way to camp out there without working plumbing if you *really* wanted."

Furious that he refused to be a Texas gentleman in this situation, Paige faced off with him once again. "That's not the point."

He let his gaze travel over her slowly from head to toe, before returning with taunting deliberation to her eyes. "The point," he guessed drolly, "is landing on top of me once again."

Paige flushed at the unbidden image Kurt's sarcastic comment brought to mind. Eager to end the exchange before he got even further under her skin, she turned her nose up. "I'd say it has been a pleasure seeing you again, Dr. McCabe…" Her voice trailed off. *But it hasn't been!*

He caught the thinly veiled insult she'd been too much of a lady to actually voice. "Same here, Dr. Chamberlain," he drawled, holding her eyes far longer than any respectable man would have. "Same here."

KURT WATCHED PAIGE STOMP back to the brand-new station wagon she had been driving of late, climb inside and slam the door.

"What happened to that sleek little red sports car she used to drive?" he asked, smiling to himself as Paige tossed her head indignantly and belted herself in.

Rowdy carried another box of pipe into Kurt's house. He walked past the floor that had been flooded by a burst pipe and entered the still intact—but currently unusable—kitchen. "I don't know. She sold it a couple of months ago and traded it in for that mom mobile."

Kurt followed with a box and set it on the floor next to a dozen others, and a stack of already unboxed drains, couplings and check valves. "Any idea why? I mean, is she dating anybody these days? On the verge of getting married or something?"

"Not that I've heard." Rowdy picked up the new disposal that was to be installed, too, and set it on the counter. "Although we don't exactly run in the same circles. She's always hanging out with the sophisticates. I tend to watch sports and play poker with the guys. Just like you." He peered at Kurt. "Why are you suddenly so interested?"

Good question. "Just trying to figure out ways to avoid her."

Rowdy hesitated. "You sure you don't want to just let her get her house fixed first?"

And let Paige think she'd harangued him into letting her jump line? Kurt folded his arms in front of him. "You've already started on mine."

"Barely. And I don't mind finishing it after hers. I can still get both places done before Christmas. Hers probably before Thanksgiving, if I get on it right away and call in some extra help."

Kurt studied his friend. "And why would I want to do that?"

"Because it'd make your life a whole lot easier?"

"In what way?" he persisted.

Rowdy headed back out to the truck to get the last load. "Listen, dude, you have to know that if you go ahead with the work on your place, you are all Paige Chamberlain is going to be talking and thinking about for the next two weeks. Heck, maybe for even longer."

Kurt grinned. "You're saying I'd be the focus of her existence?" Deep down, he wasn't opposed to that. It would make up for all the time he'd spent over the years matching wits and wills with her.

"I'm saying," Rowdy clarified with a frown, evidently still trying to get Kurt to do the right thing, "you could avoid a great big headache by being gallant and letting her go first...."

Kurt recalled the color in Paige's sculpted cheeks as they'd faced off. "I prefer having her think about me day and night."

He couldn't say what it was about Paige. Whether it was her tall, gazelle-like frame, sexy shoulders or endless legs. Or the way her glossy auburn hair framed her pretty oval face. Or even the softness of her full lips when juxtaposed against that stubborn chin. He only knew there was something about her that brought out the conqueror in him, and always had.

Only problem was, Paige Chamberlain was not the kind of woman who would ever surrender to any man.

And he definitely wanted a woman who would surrender to him. Heart, body and soul.

His beeper went off, and Kurt reached for the phone on his belt. He saw his parents' home number flash across the caller ID screen. He clicked the connect button and lifted the cell to his ear. "Hey. What's up?"

"You need to get out to the ranch right now," his mother said, sounding really irate. "You have some *serious* explaining to do!"

IT WASN'T LIKE HIS parents to get involved in the day-to-day dealings of their five sons, Kurt knew. Annie and Travis McCabe firmly believed in letting their children be held accountable for their own actions; it was, they had always maintained, the only way to teach children to be responsible adults. So Kurt found it a little hard to believe they'd be upset about the situation with Paige Chamberlain to the point they'd call him on the carpet about it. On the other hand, Annie and Paige's mom, Dani, were friends.

And Kurt wouldn't put it past Paige to call her mother and complain.

Dani, who was very protective of her only daughter, *might* have called to talk to Annie, and see if there was anything the two moms could do to eliminate even more controversy.

Still, it wasn't like his normally imperturbable mother to call, bark an order and hang up on him.

So something else had to be going on.

Something that in some way involved him, Kurt figured.

He found out what that was the moment he strolled through the door of the ranch house at the Triple Diamond.

His mother and father were there. Standing next to the biggest, most expensive-looking navy blue baby buggy Kurt had ever seen.

"We'd like an explanation," Annie McCabe said, her petite, well-dressed frame vibrating with emotion.

No joke! So would Kurt.

Travis put a comforting hand on his wife's shoulder. "Let's let him read the letter first," he said. Kurt's father walked past the baby buggy and handed over an envelope with Kurt's name scrawled across the front. It hadn't been opened.

"It came with the baby buggy," Annie explained, in response to Kurt's obvious confusion.

He frowned, ripped open the seal and read the words typed on the page out loud. "'Dear Kurt, please be the daddy Lindsay, Lori and Lucille need, and welcome them into the McCabe clan.'"

He shook his head in an attempt to clear it, and looked up, half afraid he might already know the answer to the question he was about to ask. "Who are Lindsay, Lori and Lucille?"

Annie wheeled the buggy over to where he was standing.

He looked down to see three gorgeous babies, all in pink, snuggled under a crocheted blanket, sleeping soundly. Matching gold ID bracelets, engraved with their names and some sort of filigreed design along the edges, glinted on their tiny wrists. "We were hoping," Annie said softly, "you would be able to tell us that!"

"WHOA," PAIGE SAID, as Mitzy Martin turned her car beneath the archway of the Triple Diamond Ranch. "You didn't tell me the babies were found here." Otherwise, Paige wouldn't have been so quick to volunteer to come out and examine the abandoned triplets and make sure they were all okay. Although initial reports indicated that they were in good health.

"Is it a problem?" the vivacious social worker asked.

Paige supposed not. After all, this ranch was owned

by Annie and Travis McCabe, who were great people, unlike their incorrigible son Kurt....

She pulled herself together. "No."

"One of these days," Mitzy continued with a wry smile, "you're going to have to sit down with me and explain what it is about Kurt McCabe that gets you going every time his name is even mentioned."

Paige wasn't sure she could explain that to her best friend. All she really knew was whenever the two of them came across each other, sparks flew. It didn't matter where they were or what they were doing or who else they were with. The world narrowed to just the two of them. And all she could take in was the McCabe-blue hue of his gorgeous eyes, and the wicked slant to his devilishly sexy smile. Maybe because he never once, even for an instant, seemed to stop challenging her. Truth be told, he unnerved her to the point that it took everything she had to continue to go toe-to-toe with him. Even more daunting was the delicate, feminine way he made her five-foot-eleven body feel, when confronted with his ultramasculine presence and broad-shouldered, six-foot-five frame. Like she was ripe for the picking. When she knew that just wasn't true! She was independent—to a fault....

Kurt McCabe was the kind of man women swooned over. And never snagged. Not for long, anyway...

Whereas Paige was in the market for permanence at this stage in her life. Family. Children of her very own, to nurture and love.

"You really need to tell me what it is about him that gets you so hot and bothered," Mitzy said with a wink.

"Not tonight," Paige replied as the social worker parked in front of the large stone-and-wood ranch house. Tonight, she wanted to do her job and run.

Not that Kurt McCabe was likely to be here.

He was probably in town, or out on some emergency vet call....

The massive door opened before they could even ring. Annie McCabe stood there. Dressed in tailored wool slacks, a fitted jacket and cashmere sweater, her hair upswept, Paige thought she looked every inch the successful entrepreneur. Perhaps just back from a business trip, because behind her, in a corner of the entryway, were a matching set of expensive luggage and two handsome leather briefcases. Piled on top of them were two lightweight raincoats, perfect for the changeable November weather. What a way to return home from a weeklong business trip, Paige thought.

Annie McCabe shook Mitzy's hand and engulfed Paige in a warm hug. "Thank you both for getting out here so quickly," she said.

"No problem," Paige replied.

"Is this where you found the babies?" Mitzy asked.

"On the front porch, yes," Annie confirmed. "I was upstairs when I heard the doorbell. By the time I got down here, the car was already at the end of the drive. All I saw was a pair of taillights. I couldn't even tell you what kind of vehicle it was."

Behind them, a Laramie County sheriff's car pulled up in the drive.

Deputy Detective Kyle McCabe—Kurt's identical twin brother—stepped out from behind the wheel.

Paige had always liked the kindhearted lawman, and

she smiled as he greeted the women and swiftly brought them up to speed.

"Was there a note?" Mitzy asked.

"Yes," Annie confirmed as she led the way from the foyer, down a long hall, to the comfortable family room at the rear of the residence. Dominated by a huge stone fireplace and hearth, it sported man-size upholstered furniture, lots of books, and in the center of the built-in shelving, a large wall-mounted, big-screen television.

Kurt was there, standing next to a large, navy blue English-style pram, and looking a lot less cocky than when Paige had seen him an hour earlier.

Annie continued, her expression sober, "It was addressed to Kurt."

He stepped away from the baby buggy as the three women neared. His feelings about Paige's presence here were not evident. With a look of surprising concern and maturity on his ruggedly handsome face, he turned his glance away.

Her heartbeat accelerating, Paige peered beneath the bonnet of the buggy, along with Mitzy and Annie McCabe.

Paige saw a lot of babies in her line of work, and they were all special and wonderful in their own unique way. But these three infants were absolutely adorable. And identical. With tufts of dark, curly hair peeking out from matching pink crocheted caps, sweet, cherubic faces and big blue eyes that radiated wonder, they would have won a Beautiful Baby contest hands down.

Which made the idea that anyone would abandon them even more unfathomable. Especially when everything about their physical appearance and demeanor said they had been extremely well cared for prior to this.

Without thinking, Paige turned to Kurt. She noted he still looked as disconcerted as she now felt. "Is it possible these triplets are yours?"

He stood motionless, almost in shock. "I don't know," he muttered finally.

Paige locked eyes with him, not sure why she cared, just knowing she did. "But could they be?" she pressed.

Kurt's jaw tightened. "Yes."

Chapter Two

Kyle McCabe turned to his twin, in full detective mode. "You said there was a note?"

"I'd like to see it, too," Mitzy remarked.

Kurt handed it over. Though Paige didn't ask, it was given to her to peruse, too. She was sure Kurt would have preferred she not see it, and probably not even be there to witness this stunning event. Normally, Kurt McCabe liked to play his cards close to his chest and keep his personal business private. But in this case, they all needed any illumination they could get. And as one of three pediatricians in town, Paige was as likely as anyone to be able to come up with a clue.

"There's no signature," she murmured, feeling even more perplexed after reading the cryptic plea. What drove a woman to leave her three babies parked on someone's front porch on a cold November night? Why wouldn't the infants' mother have contacted Kurt, or someone in his family, directly? Especially since the McCabes were known throughout Texas for their up-standing character and devotion to children?

"There doesn't need to be a name on it," Kurt muttered.

Everyone turned to look at him.

"If I'm the father, and I'm still having a little trouble believing that I am," he continued shortly, "there's only one possibility."

The tall, effortlessly sexy Kurt McCabe and baby making were two things that did not need to be put together in Paige's mind. She drew a deep breath and pushed the image of him—naked, between the sheets— from her thoughts.

"Have you spoken to Camila Albright?" Kyle asked his brother as he removed a pad and pen from his pocket.

Without warning, Paige began to flush.

Noticing her reaction, Kurt wordlessly furrowed his brow. He turned back to his brother. "I've already tried to phone Camila twice. She's not returning my calls. But then—" he shrugged his broad shoulders and rubbed a palm across the back of his neck "—it's been that way since we broke up."

Kyle was silent, obviously thinking. "Which was when, exactly?" He scribbled notes as he talked.

His twin's mouth twitched at the corner. "Last fall."

"And you had no indication she was pregnant?"

Kurt's lips thinned even more. "None," he said, staring straight ahead.

Silence fell. Kurt offered nothing more. The babies began to stir. Wondering if Kurt McCabe would be more forthcoming with the authorities if she wasn't there to witness everything he said, Paige interjected, "Maybe I should take a look at the babies now."

Already backtracking toward the front of the house, Kyle removed his phone from its leather holder. "I'll check and see if there are any infants reported missing," the handsome detective said.

"And I'll see what I can find out on my end," Mitzy promised, going in yet another direction and plucking her phone from her purse.

Kurt's mother jumped into action. "I'll give you a hand with the little ones." She beckoned for Paige to follow her as she turned the buggy around, pushed it out of the family room, down another hall in the rambling one-story house, and into the wing where the bedrooms were housed. Annie wheeled the babies into a guest room and parked the buggy next to an elegantly made-up queen-size bed. "Thanks for coming over on such short notice, Paige."

She opened up her satchel and removed her stethoscope. "It's my job." Just as it was her job now not to get emotionally involved in the situation.

"They're beautiful, aren't they?" Annie said softly as they lifted all three girls out of the buggy and laid them side by side near the center of the bed.

"Very," Paige murmured.

And one day, she thought, if she was very lucky, she would have a little girl, too.

In the meantime, it was up to her to see to the health of the three babies in front of her. And putting her own empathetic feelings aside, that was exactly what she would do.

KURT SPENT THE NEXT FEW minutes alternately pacing and staring out the windows at the front of the ranch house, as if doing so would bring the perpetrator of this event back to her senses. Part of him couldn't believe this was actually happening, and yet…hadn't he secretly wanted a family of his own for what seemed like forever? But to get it this way, under such mysterious circumstances, left him feeling unsettled. He did not enjoy the sensation of his life fast spiraling out of control. That kind of emotional chaos was for others, not for him. He liked things light and easy. Not overwrought, and full of drama that could easily have been avoided….

Without warning, Kurt felt a warm hand clasp his shoulder. Grateful for the show of solidarity and comfort, he turned. Sympathy radiated in his father's eyes. "You doing okay?" Travis asked quietly.

Kurt wasn't sure how to answer that. He looked at Mitzy Martin, who was standing in the dining room, talking on her cell phone, and at his brother Kyle, who was sitting outside in his squad car, doing the same.

Finally, Kurt shrugged. "I'd feel a heck of a lot better if I knew for certain what was being said in both those conversations." He understood his brother asking a pediatrician to come out and examine the kids. That only made sense. But as for the rest of the brouhaha currently going on… "Why is the social worker here?" he asked, feeling even more tense.

"Kyle said it's standard procedure in situations like this," Travis said.

Of course Kurt's law-and-order twin would think that way. "But if the babies are mine…shouldn't this be a private family matter? Something for my lawyer and hers to figure out?" he asked.

Mitzy joined them in time to interject, "I know what the note implied, but we have no proof right now that these are your babies, Kurt."

That sounded like bureaucratic hooey to him. "We have no proof they aren't, either," he retorted. And that being the case, he wanted to proceed as if the triplets were his, and give them every protection possible.

Paige and Annie turned the corner and wheeled the buggy down the broad hall that ran the length of the home. Kurt could tell by the looks on the two women's faces as they approached that they'd both heard what Mitzy had said.

Feeling a little like a father waiting for news outside the delivery room, Kurt turned to Paige. "How are the babies?" And why was that lump suddenly in his throat?

She smiled. "They're all in perfect health. They seem well cared for, a nice healthy weight."

That was a relief. Kurt exhaled slowly, then asked, "How old would you say they are?"

Paige lifted a hand. "Three months, give or take."

Which meant, Kurt thought, Camila Albright could have delivered them. The timing would have been right, if she'd gotten pregnant shortly before they'd stopped seeing each other. But if that was the case, why hadn't Camila contacted him? Why would she have gone through something like that alone, especially when giving birth to triplets? It didn't make sense.

Kyle came back in. "Anything on your end?" Mitzy asked him in a crisp tone.

He shook his head. "No reports of missing triplets anywhere in the nation, thus far. Of course it's early... given they were just dropped off an hour or so ago."

"So now what?" Kurt asked impatiently, wondering how this had gotten so bureaucratic so fast.

"The babies are going into foster care," Mitzy said.

"What?" Kurt, Annie and Travis cried in unison.

Kyle backed Mitzy up. "It's standard procedure for abandoned babies."

Kurt looked at his brother. Most of the time he and his twin got along famously. Other times, like now... "Somehow, I don't think you would be suggesting this if these babies might be yours.…" Kurt told him.

"Actually," Kyle said, his by-the-book side emerging as strongly as Kurt's one-day-at-a-time attitude. "I would, for a lot of different reasons. For starters, you've got no running water, and you can't expect the babies to bunk at the vet clinic in the meantime, the way you have been. Second, you know zilch about caring for babies. And third, this could all be a scam, brought about by someone interested in a piece of the McCabe family fortune." He shrugged. "So until we know otherwise... I'm not sure it would be wise for any of us to get too attached."

Easier said than done, Kurt thought, looking over at the triplets, who were cuddled together in the pram once again.

The three baby girls held the emotional appeal of newborn puppies. And everyone knew Kurt had always been a total sucker for puppies. It was why he'd become a general practice vet who took care of small animals as well as horses and cattle.

Mitzy lifted a staying hand. "It's just until we get this straightened out and figure out who the birth parents are. If Lori, Lindsay and Lucille are indeed your biological children, Kurt, we'll recommend family court recognize you as their legal father and award you immediate temporary custody. But until then, we have to follow the rules. Now, do you want the good news or the bad news first?"

Kurt wasn't sure it could get any worse. "The bad," he said with a beleaguered sigh.

"All the foster homes in the surrounding counties are full. So our option is to split them up, ship one to Dallas, one to Houston and the third to Corpus Christi."

Out of the corner of his eye, Kurt saw Paige's eyes widen in dismay. At least, he thought grimly, the two of them agreed on something. Hoping the pediatrician would use whatever sway she had with social services and back him up, he said, "That's unacceptable." Foster care for *his kids?* "I can take them."

Unfortunately for him, Paige seemed to have as many doubts about that as her social worker friend. So much for enlisting the good doctor's help, he thought.

Mitzy gave him a long-suffering smile. "Believe me, I understand that your heart is in the right place, Kurt, and if I were you I'd probably feel the same way. But you're not a foster parent."

So what? He was a McCabe, and if there was one thing McCabes understood, it was devotion to family. "I can still care for them," he insisted.

"Not without undergoing foster parent training first. Which brings me to the good news!" Mitzy beamed like a scientist who had just come across the perfect solution to a thorny problem. "Paige does have the required training. She took it while in medical school."

Kurt glanced at Paige, whose cheeks had turned a bright pink. "I took those classes to better understand my patients and their families!" she declared, avoiding his eyes as she swung back around to face her friend. "I never intended to actually foster a child!"

Mitzy lifted her hands as if the matter was already settled. "What can I say? The universe works in mysterious ways. We need you to help us out here, Paige, at least through the weekend. And I'm sure Kurt and indeed the whole McCabe family would appreciate it if you did." She paused and gazed at her friend. Something significant—and mysterious—passed between them. "Think of it is as good practice," she finished with a wink and a smile.

Practice for what? Kurt wondered.

Was Paige pregnant?

Her flat belly seemed to indicate otherwise.

He dragged his gaze back to her face as Mitzy continued pressuring her with the unerring resolve for which she was known. "So what do you say, Paige? I know you're off until Monday. I already checked the call schedule at the hospital."

Paige stood there, silent.

Was she really his only option? Kurt wondered.

It appeared so.

Tired of sitting on the sidelines, doing nothing, while everyone else worked to resolve what was in fact his problem, he jumped in. Not bothering to mask his impatience, he strode forward and demanded, "Well, Paige? Are you willing to help out or not?"

THERE WERE DOZENS OF reasons why Paige should say no, starting with Kurt McCabe's supremely overbearing attitude. And there were also three little reasons why she should say yes. All of whom were staring at her from the buggy where they'd been tenderly resettled.

"I'd love to help out, temporarily, but I have nowhere to care for them," Paige said, glad she had an excuse not to become even more emotionally involved in this situation than she already was. She offered the brisk smile she gave to parents of patients when she had to deliver not so great news. "Thanks to a delay in the plumbing repairs at my house, I have no running water, either, so…"

"Not a problem!" Annie clapped her hands together enthusiastically. "You can stay here at our ranch!"

Her husband's broad shoulders relaxed in relief. "Works for me," Travis said.

"We've got plenty of room," Annie continued, taking charge of "her brood"—and anyone else who happened to be in her children's orbit—the way she always had. "And Kurt can stay here, too, and help."

Paige didn't dispute that more than one grown-up would be required to take care of three-month-old triplets. Even then it would likely be a Herculean task. But Annie and Travis had parented one set of triplets and a pair of twins, and with them around it would be easier.

Realizing that she would be more of a figurehead foster mom than anything else, there to satisfy the bureaucratic requirements of the unusual situation, Paige really didn't have to think about it further. It was the right thing to do, for the kids' sakes.

As the silence stretched out, everyone turned to Mitzy to get her opinion on Annie McCabe's suggestion.

"Actually, that's probably a very good idea," the social

worker decided, after a long, thoughtful moment. "But it's just for the weekend," she stipulated hurriedly, once again warning the McCabes not to get too attached to the three adorable baby girls just yet. "In the meantime, I'll continue working my end."

"And I'll continue keeping an eye out for any reports about abandoned or kidnapped children from law enforcement," Kyle said.

Mitzy looked at Kurt. "You keep trying to get in touch with Camila Albright."

"Will do," he promised.

Although he wasn't sure how quickly he could accomplish that. The elusive screenwriter could be hard to contact even when she wasn't ticked off at him, as she was now.

"In the meantime, we'll all keep in close touch by phone, so we can let each other know if any problems come up or other information is revealed." Mitzy finished packing up.

"Or if the mother contacts Kurt," Paige added.

Mitzy nodded, as if she half expected that to happen, too. She looked at Travis and Annie, explaining, "This could all be a ploy to get Kurt to own up to his responsibility."

"There are easier ways to do that," he said, increasingly impatient to get the situation resolved. "Like simply telling me I'm a dad." He didn't know why he felt prodded to announce this—he just did, "I would have done the right thing. No question."

"No one in the room thinks otherwise," Annie told her son quietly.

Except perhaps Paige Chamberlain, Kurt noted.

Who prior to this moment had held a very low opinion of him. A low opinion he had gone out of his way to substantiate—all so he could have the satisfaction of getting to her, again and again.

But the petty rivalry between him and Paige was irrelevant now. They were no longer students competing for everything from valedictorian—which she'd won by a mere tenth of a point—to the top science prize, to who would get repairs done on their home first. The well-being of the triplets was of paramount importance to both of them now.

"What if Camila doesn't show up?" Kurt said, more certain than ever the babies were his. They had to be! Otherwise, Camila never would have left them here.

Mitzy plucked a pad from her bag and made a note. "Then I suggest we all meet back here at noon on Monday so we can figure out where we go from here."

"Sounds good," Kurt said. Because there was no way he was going to continue to let someone else be responsible for these children, if they were his. These three little girls deserved better than being left on someone's doorstep. A whole lot better.

At the very least they should know they were wanted.

And safe.

And worth fighting for.

As if oblivious to the protective nature of his brother's thoughts, Kyle turned to Mitzy, one public servant to another. "I'll walk you out."

"Wait!" Paige cried. "I don't have my car here or any clothes!"

Mitzy clapped a hand to her forehead, looking

chagrined. "Of course. I'll give you a ride back into town so you can get your things together."

"In the meantime..." Paige turned to Annie and Travis, a question in her eyes.

Kurt wasn't surprised Paige didn't trust him to care for the triplets on his own. Any more than she trusted him in any other realm. But her lack of confidence in his parenting abilities still aggravated him.

Kurt's mother stepped in. "We'll hold the fort down here and care for the girls until you get back," she promised with a reassuring smile.

And that, Kurt noted, was that.

"NEED SOME HELP carrying things in?" Travis McCabe asked when Paige got back to the Triple Diamond Ranch an hour later.

She set her medical bag and purse in the front hall. "Actually, that would be very nice." She cocked her head. "How are things going?" She didn't hear any commotion.

Travis held the front door for her. "You can see for yourself, as soon as we're done."

They walked together to the station wagon, parked in the circular drive in front of the house. "Looks like you're prepared for any eventuality," he teased as Paige opened the hatch.

She flushed. She wasn't sure she had remembered half the items she would need for herself during her weekend stay at the Triple Diamond, but she had done okay on the baby front. "I stopped off to get diapers and formula before I left town."

"Good thinking." Travis took her suitcase and tucked

two boxes of diapers under his arm. Paige grabbed the sacks of formula and her laptop computer.

"Thanks for helping us out here," he said.

She shrugged. "I was glad to do it." Maybe not so glad to have to reside under the same roof as Kurt McCabe, but it wouldn't be too bad with his parents there to keep him on his very best behavior and run interference between them. "I didn't want to see the triplets split up, either. They're probably traumatized enough."

"They aren't acting that way," Travis remarked, leading the way back inside. "But then, maybe you should see for yourself."

They set their cache down and headed to the family room.

Annie was seated in an overstuffed armchair, a triplet in each arm. Kurt was seated in the rocking chair. Annie looked perfectly at ease, juggling two babies. Kurt looked hard-pressed and awkward handling just one.

Paige breathed a sigh of relief that they had so much help. Although she routinely examined babies, she had no experience taking care of them.

"Ready to go, hon?" Travis asked his wife.

Paige froze.

Looking really reluctant to let either infant go, Annie made a face.

"We need to get to Dallas if we want to catch any sleep before our flight tomorrow morning," her husband prodded.

Kurt's head shot up. "What are you talking about?" he demanded.

Apparently, he was as stunned as she was by the announcement, Paige noted.

"We're going to be in California for the next six days," Travis said. "We're not returning to Texas until early Thanksgiving Day."

Annie added with a smile, "Annie's Homemade is being picked up by a large grocery store chain on the West Coast, and we're in talks with several others."

Paige wasn't surprised to hear that. Mrs. McCabe's brand of barbecue sauces, jams and jellies were delicious. All had been famous in Texas for years.

Panic etched the handsome lines of Kurt's face. "You didn't say anything about leaving tonight!" he protested.

Paige knew exactly how he felt.

"I'm pretty sure we mentioned it at least half a dozen times over the last month." Annie handed over one of the babies to Travis, then stood. Together, they settled the two girls side by side in the buggy, then gestured for Kurt to do the same.

Gingerly, he got up and crossed the short distance. Rather than put her in the buggy himself, he handed the third baby off to his mother, then watched as she expertly settled her, so the three of them were nestled shoulder to shoulder beneath the crocheted pink blanket. "I meant tonight," Kurt murmured quietly.

Annie jiggled the buggy slightly, moving it back and forth in a somnolent motion. "We were a little distracted," she said in her own defense.

"The fact is," Travis interjected calmly, "your mother and I are on the 6:00 a.m. flight out of DFW tomorrow, and we have reservations at an airport hotel. So now that the babies are all fed and changed, we really need to get going. I'm sure the two of you can handle it from here," he added rather impatiently.

Could they? Paige wondered.

Chapter Three

"Don't look at me like that," Kurt said the moment he and Paige were alone.

She slipped off her brown suede jacket and ivory scarf, and draped them neatly over the back of a chair. Then lifted a slender eyebrow in a way that let him know she had her dander up. "Like what?" she asked crisply.

"Like this is somehow to my benefit," he retorted. "I had no idea this was coming."

Paige shrugged her slender shoulders. "Given your less-than-enthusiastic reaction, I figured as much."

He waited. "Then…?"

Paige glared at him, temper flashing in her eyes. "You have to admit the thought of both of us under the same roof for an entire weekend is a little off-putting."

"No argument there," Kurt agreed.

"Fortunately…" Paige headed back to the foyer, where she'd left the belongings she'd brought in with her. She picked up the briefcase and pulled out a bundle of papers. "We're going to be a little busy." She separated the pages and handed half to him.

Seeing the regimented-to-a-fault part of Paige he had

most loathed in his youth, Kurt sighed and looked down at the printout. "What's this?" Did he really want to know?

She flashed a patronizing smile. "It's the set of instructions I give new parents. I left off the first couple of pages, because obviously we're past the newborn stage here. I thought we'd pick up with the three-month information."

Many things came to Kurt's mind, none of them fit for a lady's ears. "You're kidding, right?"

She clamped her arms in front of her, the action drawing his attention to the soft curves of her breasts.

"The triplets need to be on a schedule, if they're not already."

Kurt turned his glance toward the trio of cute little babies, cuddled together as snugly as newborn pups, and looking just as content. "They seem to be doing fine to me."

Paige huffed out an exasperated breath. "They're sleeping!"

"Well, duh."

"It's eight-thirty in the evening."

What did that matter? "Which, as it happens, is past *my* dinner hour," Kurt told her.

Briefly, Paige looked as if she wanted to pull her hair out in frustration. "Mine, too, but that's hardly the point, Dr. McCabe."

Irritated to find her going back to their previous formality, Kurt replied sarcastically, "Given the way my stomach is grumbling, that's exactly the point, Dr. Chamberlain!"

Paige tossed her head, like the diva-esque Southern

belle she had never been. "Do you want to sleep through the night tonight or not?"

Kurt found himself tracking the fall of auburn hair caressing the feminine lines of her face. Wondering if it was as silky to the touch as it looked, he asked, "Is that a rhetorical question?"

She sent him a chastising look. "I'm serious."

So was he. He was also tired of playing these guessing games. Why did he always feel as if the two of them were talking different languages? "Yes, Paige, I want to sleep through the night," he huffed impatiently.

"Then we're going to have to wake up the triplets."

Talk about dumb ideas! Kurt made no effort to hide his mounting exasperation. "And why is that, pray tell?"

Paige rolled her eyes. "Because babies this age typically sleep six to eight hours straight, once they are put down for the night. And if the triplets think they are down for the night now, they'll be wide-awake and raring to go at two in the morning. So unless you want to be up all night, playing with them..." She offered a polite smile and left the question hanging.

He did not.

Trying not to overreact to her bossiness, Kurt folded his arms in front of him. Pushing away the idea of shocking the heck out of her and kissing her into silence, he asked with exaggerated politeness, "What did you have in mind?"

"First, that we figure out where they're going to sleep tonight, and get that set up."

Kurt reminded himself that she was a pediatrician, and claimed to know what she was doing here. Deciding to let her call the shots—for now—he shrugged. "I thought they'd be in with you."

Paige looked him in the eye. "Babies do better in their own room. And since I presume you've got the space here to provide a temporary nursery...?"

Kurt took another look at the infants, who were still all sleeping soundly, side by side in the buggy, then headed for the wing of the large rambling ranch house where the bedrooms were located. He passed the master suite, then came to the first of half a dozen guest rooms, and gestured down the hall. "Take your pick."

She ambled past him. As she surveyed the rooms, he couldn't help but survey her.

When Paige had gone home, she'd changed out of her work clothes and into something more comfortable. She now wore a pair of dark denim jeans and a V-neck cashmere sweater that clung to her softly rounded breasts and brought out the emerald green of her wide-set eyes. She'd put on a pair of stack-heeled Western boots that added another two inches to her already considerable height. He remembered her glossy, auburn hair as being curly when she was a kid, but these days sleek, full layers framed her oval face and gave her a look of sophisticated professionalism.

Everything about her said she lived a life that was fully under her control. And everything about him wanted to unfurl that control and find the untamed woman underneath.

If she wasn't such an argumentative know-it-all, he might have been tempted to pay attention to the pull of attraction simmering just beneath the surface of every interaction they had.

But that's who she was, he reminded himself. And now that they had three kids to take care of, it was probably best to just concentrate on surviving the weekend, and disregard any foolish notions about taming Paige....

Clearly oblivious to the ardent nature of his thoughts, Paige wrapped up her tour of the guest rooms and turned back to him. "How about these three bedrooms over here, since they all connect? We can put the triplets in the middle, with you on one side and me on the other. That way we'll be sure to hear them when they wake up in the night."

"I thought we were going to try and make sure they didn't wake up in the middle of the night."

Paige shot him a quick, reproving glance. "*Try* being the operative word. Now, the next question is, do you have a baby bathtub?"

How would he know? He was a single guy in a family that boasted many capable women, and his mother—the lady of this household—wasn't here. "I'm going to say no."

Paige studied the shallow sinks in the hall bathroom, then headed back toward the kitchen. She stood, hands on her hips, surveying the marble counters and the wide farmhouse sink. "This is better. Let's do it here."

Kurt's stomach grumbled. He looked longingly at the fridge, which he knew would be well stocked. "Sure you don't want to eat first?" The babies were quiet. What would be the harm?

"I'm sure," Paige stated. She eyed him consideringly from beneath her thick auburn lashes. "Can you get several plush towels and a couple of washcloths?"

That sounded an awful lot like an order to him. He dug in stubbornly. *"Please."*

She flushed, inhaled loudly, and repeated, "Please."

Wondering if this was how henpecked husbands felt, Kurt nodded in victory and strode off. En route to the linen closet, he detoured to check on the triplets. They were still sleeping soundly.

Too bad that wouldn't last...

When he came back, Paige had three sets of clothing laid out. Shampoo, baby wash and lotion from a starter baby bath kit were all neatly lined up. Sleeves rolled to her elbow, she was busy filling the sink with several inches of water. "Okay, let's get the first one," she said cheerfully.

As Kurt had predicted, Lucille was none too happy to be awakened. And even less pleased to find herself disrobed and lowered into a lukewarm bath. The minute her skin touched the water, she set up a wail that could have been heard three counties over.

"Now, now," Paige soothed, trying to hold on to the flailing, squalling infant.

What looked so easy when others did it, Kurt noted, was not easy at all. Paige spared him a quick glance over her shoulder, as the other two awakened and also began to cry. "Can you give me a hand here?"

He wanted the crying to stop, too. The sound was breaking his heart. "What do you want me to do?" he asked anxiously.

She continued without much success to try to soothe the bawling infant. "Can you wash her hair?" she asked above the din.

Kurt looked at the fragile little form and felt his

normal confidence ebb. "How about I hold her and you do the washing?"

Giving Paige no chance to disagree, he moved to take over. Their arms brushed as he stepped in close and slid one hand beneath Lucille's thrashing body, the other beneath her neck and head. Lucille's expression changed slightly, as if she knew something was different now, but couldn't figure out exactly what.

Taking advantage of her momentary inaction, Paige put a dollop of baby wash on her palm and rubbed it across the wet infant, sudsing her gently and quickly, then used an even smaller dollop of shampoo on her scalp.

That went over about as well as the initial dip in the lukewarm water. Lucille immediately increased her crying to top volume once again. Her expression pediatrician-calm and focused, Paige rinsed the baby with the drenched washcloth and reached for a towel. Kurt handed Lucille over and Paige wrapped her up. Indignant, and probably hungry now, too, the child continued to scream.

Her two sisters chorused right along with her.

"Now what?" Kurt asked.

"If you can dress Lucille, I'll bathe—" Paige lifted the second baby from the buggy and checked out her bracelet "—Lori."

"You sure you can do it all by yourself?"

"I'm going to have to try."

As it turned out, Paige couldn't bathe Lori all by herself, any more than Kurt could seem to get the sleeper on the uncooperative Lucille. So he ended up wrapping

Lucille in a towel again and setting her down in the buggy next to her still howling sister Lindsay, and going back over to help Paige bathe Lori. When they finished with her, Lori was put back in the buggy, and Lindsay got her bath.

Once that was done, Paige—who turned out to have better diapering and dressing skills—got one at a time into sleepers, while Kurt pushed the buggy around in a vain attempt to quiet the other two.

Finally, everyone was dressed—and still crying. "Now what?" Kurt said.

For the first time he could recall, Paige had no ready answers. Looking as if she might burst into tears at any second herself, she rushed to get the papers she'd brought in with her, and read over them quickly.

"I don't know," she said finally. "How long has it been since they ate?"

At last, some common sense! Kurt checked his watch. "Two hours ago—I think." Too late, he realized he should have been paying closer attention while his mom and dad were still here. Then again, when they were here, he hadn't yet known he and Paige would be doing all the "parenting" this weekend, without their help and expertise.

Paige tapped her foot as she continued studying the handout. "They shouldn't be hungry for another hour or two."

"Well, we have to do something," Kurt insisted.

She looked at the supplies that had come from beneath the buggy and now lay scattered about. "Do you see any pacifiers?"

Kurt felt around the edges of the buggy, then got

down on his knees to search through the basket under-neath. "Nothing. I don't suppose you brought any with you?"

Paige looked chagrined. "Nope."

"Then I guess we're going to have to soothe them the old-fashioned way," he said.

He picked up Lucille and settled her against his right shoulder. "Hand me Lori," he directed. Then he swiftly cradled her against the center of his chest, the way he had seen his mom and dad both do. It was a bit awkward, but it felt good to be holding the babies in his arms, even if they were still crying.

Paige took Lindsay. "Now what?" she asked, a slightly panicked look on her face as she patted the wailing infant on the back.

"We walk." Kurt had to shout to be heard as he headed off in the opposite direction. "And sing."

AN HOUR AND COUNTLESS songs later, all three babies were asleep and settled back in the buggy. It was ten o'clock. Paige looked as if she had been through the wringer. Kurt felt the same.

"You realize we're going to have to wake and feed them again in the next hour," Paige said. "And to do that we have to find the bottles, wash them and prepare formula."

This time, Kurt did not intend to ignore the rumbling of his empty stomach. "All the more reason why you and I need to eat something now."

For once Paige didn't argue with him. She simply dragged herself into the kitchen and took a seat at the table. Then buried her face in her hands. "I don't suppose you have any cold cereal?"

Kurt looked at her in satisfaction. Finally, she was listening to him. "I think we can do better than that," he assured her.

Paige waved a hand. "Cold cereal is fine. I eat it for dinner all the time when I have to work late."

"Sounds...Spartan."

"Cold cereal can be very comforting after a long, hard day."

"Or night," Kurt quipped. She rewarded him with a wan smile. He saw the vulnerability in her expression and wished he had some way to make this easier for all of them, without admitting it might be too much for them to handle. "Then cold cereal it is." He ambled to the pantry to study the well-stocked shelves. "We have bran flakes, raisin bran, all bran and cracklin' bran...."

Paige's soft laughter sprang up between them. She sat back in her chair, smiling now. "I'm sensing a theme here."

"Apparently so." Kurt scratched his head. "My parents used to have a wider selection." Finally, he brought out bran flakes and raisin bran and set them on the large oak table.

He went back to get bowls and spoons.

She tilted her head, looking at him curiously. "You don't eat breakfast here often?"

He set the dishes down in front of her, then returned to the fridge to get milk, grabbing the sugar bowl on the way back. "Not unless it's a family thing...and when we all gather around my mom goes all out, with omelets and biscuits and gravy, you name it." Sitting down kitty-corner from Paige, Kurt watched her shake raisin bran into her bowl and sprinkle on a little extra sugar.

Interesting. They both liked their cereal the same way.

"What about you?" He watched as she liberally poured on the milk. "Eating breakfast at your folks' ranch much since you've been back?"

Paige shook her head and took a bite. "Not unless I'm staying there between houses or something."

"Between houses?"

The long-suffering look she gave him reminded him that although she had been back in Laramie for close to three years now, practicing pediatric medicine, he had been working and residing there for only two months. Which was yet another way she had an edge over him.

Paige chased the last raisin with a spoon and then shook more cereal into her bowl, filling it up to the brim once again. "The Victorian I'm living in now is my third. I buy and fix them up and then sell them and move on."

Kurt couldn't say he was surprised about that. Paige always had been ambitious to a fault. Always putting hard work above the simple act of enjoying herself. He hadn't even begun decorating the house he was living in.

He finished his bowl of cereal and got up to peruse the fridge. "No interest in the finished product?"

"Once I get it perfect, there's nothing more for me to do."

Kurt came back to the table with a bowl of chilled clementines. "And you like things perfect."

He was acutely aware of her as she watched him peel

off the deep orange skin and break one into sections. He felt her undivided attention as surely as a caress.

Their eyes met and locked, provoking another wave of heat between them. She accepted a sliver of orange, her fingers briefly brushing his before pulling away. "Don't you?"

"No." Kurt savored the sweet flavor of the fruit on his tongue. "For me, the more imperfect something is, the better."

"Why is that?" She reached for a clementine and began to peel it in turn.

"I don't know." He attempted to defend his position. "I think it's more like real life."

Still listening, she leaned close enough that he could inhale the faint lavender fragrance of her perfume. "Hmm."

He looked at the sterling silver lotus flower pendant shimmering against her skin. Lower still, he could see the hint of cleavage at the open V of her cashmere sweater. Damning the growing pressure at the front of his jeans, he forced his attention back to her face and surveyed her in his trademark challenging way. "Obviously you don't agree."

Her green eyes sparked with indignation. "Don't act surprised," she retorted. "You and I don't agree on much of anything."

Why was he suddenly wishing that were otherwise? He shrugged. "True."

Paige neatly stacked the discarded orange peel in her empty bowl and carried it to the sink. Kurt waited for her to run the garbage disposal. When she had finished, the fragrance of clementines filled the air.

"Although," she added, strolling back to the table to collect the cereal boxes and put them away, too, "I must say you surprised me here today, taking responsibility the way you have, for these three kids."

Irritation sprang up within him, as surely as desire had. "What would you have expected me to do?"

"I don't know." Paige paced back and forth restlessly. "Immediately ask for a DNA test and wait for a positive result before claiming any responsibility, I guess."

Kurt couldn't think of a more colossal waste of time, under the circumstances. "Who does that?" he demanded.

"My ex-fiancé."

Kurt wanted to think she was kidding. The pained expression on her face said she was not.

He trod carefully. "I didn't know you were engaged."

Sorrow flickered briefly in her eyes. She kept her distance, lounging against the sink. "It was one of those fast, impetuous things that never should have happened, and probably only did because of the arduous situation we found ourselves in during our first year of med school." Another shadow crossed her face. "As it happened, the relationship didn't last long. I barely had time to tell my parents about our engagement before I realized I was pregnant."

Kurt studied the mixture of regret and grief in her eyes. His heart going out to her, he moved closer. "What happened?"

She gripped the counter on either side of her. A pulse throbbed in her throat. "I miscarried."

"I'm so sorry."

She accepted his condolences with a barely perceptible nod of her head. Swallowing, she averted her gaze and plunged on. "It was probably a good thing, given the fact that upon hearing the news, Neil immediately doubted his involvement in the matter and asked for a DNA test."

Kurt did a double take. "Even though you were engaged?" He was sure he couldn't have heard correctly.

Paige let out a beleaguered sigh. "Neil explained it was just a formality, due to the fact we had been dating only a couple of months. He said my pregnancy could easily be further along than either of us knew."

"Or in other words, started before he entered the scene," Kurt guessed, wanting to punch the guy.

"Right." Bitter irony edged Paige's low tone. "Naturally, I didn't see it that way."

Kurt sympathized. "I wouldn't have, either."

She lifted her chin. "The point is, Neil wasn't ready to be a father, so his first impulse was to go into denial and cite the contraception he had been diligently using. And therefore, reason that unexpected fatherhood could not be happening to him."

Kurt knew the legal system was full of guys who were doing the same thing in order to dodge responsibility. That didn't make it right. "Seems like your ex could have done that without impugning your integrity."

Silence fell. Paige offered a weak smile. "It does, doesn't it?" She shook her head, weariness descending on her delicate features once again. "Anyway, I broke up with Neil, and I haven't been serious about anyone since."

Hadn't dared to be, Kurt figured. He knew all about

calculating the odds of getting hurt again, and voting against it. "You've decided not to marry?" he guessed. For reasons he chose not to examine, he hoped that was not the case.

Her expression softened with regret. "Not unless I find my Perfect Man." Without warning, the sparkle was back in her green eyes. "And that doesn't seem likely."

He studied the challenging slant to her lips, and once again found the need to gain the upper hand. "Perfection is overrated," he murmured.

She raised a brow. "You think so?"

Kurt edged closer. "Yep." He rested his hands on her shoulders.

Paige's pretty chin set defiantly. "I don't agree." But there was no denying that small catch in her voice.

It was his turn to smile. Move in. "You might," he countered, "if you gave the imperfect a try."

He angled his head and let his face drift slowly, inevitably toward hers. As she tried to evade what was coming, they bumped noses, ever so slightly. He paused, and then she gave in to the latent curiosity that had been plaguing them both all evening, and let it happen. As he came closer, she opened her mouth slightly. His lips made contact with the silky sweetness of hers. A jolt shot through him. Needing more, he wrapped his arms around her, flattening a hand across her spine, and brought her all the way against him. The softness of her body curved into the hardness of his. Heat sifted through him. She moaned, soft and low, the woman in her urging him on, even as the cynic in her pushed him away.

Breathlessly, they moved apart.

He could tell by the glitter in her eyes and the quickness of her breath, the way her breasts pushed against the softness of her cashmere sweater, that she was every bit as aroused as he. And ticked off about it, too. Triumph roared through him. Maybe he'd finally get her to surrender to him, after all. "See, that wasn't perfect, but it wasn't bad, either."

Paige took another step back and propped her hands on her hips. "Are you hitting on me?" she demanded, as if it was the last thing she had ever expected.

He chuckled. "Afraid so."

She inhaled shakily. Lifted both palms. "We can't."

He had figured persuasion was going to be required. Lucky thing he was up to the task. "Not in the if-it-feels-good-do-it camp, hmm?" he taunted lightly.

Her auburn brows knit together. "Not even close. Even," Paige added nimbly, stepping close once again, "if I didn't know what that embrace was about."

Chapter Four

When Kurt gave her a searching glance, Paige took refuge in the obvious. "That kiss was the result of the infectious joy all new parents feel." She had seen it countless times before. "Having a baby—or in this case, having three delivered to your doorstep—leaves a person feeling so happy and excited he or she wants to kiss or hug everyone." And Kurt McCabe had eventually done just that.

It was her reaction to his understandable—if misguided—exuberance that was the problem. Caring for the infants together was an unexpectedly intimate endeavor. This weekend was beginning to feel too much like a date, with more passionate kisses in the making. And it wasn't. She would do well to remember that.

"In your case, of course," she continued ever so sweetly, falling back on the rancor that had kept her safe from the possibility of hooking up with him lo these many years, "that translated to something else."

"Such as...?" he drawled, still regarding her appreciatively.

With effort, Paige ignored the just-kissed tingling of her lips, and the tremors of excitement gathering deep inside her. "The basic human need for sex and affection." The one they all harbored, in some fashion or another. She drew a relieved breath. "Thankfully, we came to our senses and ended the ill-advised kiss." Before the situation got really out of control...

He pushed away from the wall and straightened his tall, broad-shouldered frame. "You really think that's what it was?" he said, closing the distance between them once again.

Pleased she could sound like such a prude and an utter turnoff, she nodded. "Of course." She regarded Kurt stoically, backing up until her spine hit the refrigerator. "What else could it be? We can't stand each other. Remember?"

He looked at her impatiently. "*Couldn't* stand each other," he corrected with a frown, as if he wasn't sure how he felt now.

Another thrill swept through her. "So we got along for a while this evening." She forced herself to go on what she knew to be true, rather than the way he was behaving. "That feeling of camaraderie can't last—and it won't, since I'll be caring for the babies just for the weekend. Come Monday morning, roughly thirty-six hours from now, they're going to be either in your care or someone else's." Paige would be out of the picture completely. "Speaking of which," she forced herself to add matter-of-factly, "have you heard back from Camila Albright yet?"

Kurt removed the cell phone from the leather case on his belt. He checked through the messages. "Nothing." He sighed in obvious frustration. "And I've called her half a dozen times."

"Is that the only way she would've tried to contact you—on your cell?"

"If she wanted to talk to me, yeah."

"And if she doesn't…?"

He nodded. "Good point. She might have sent an email. But I don't have my computer."

Glad for the diversion, Paige offered, "You can borrow my laptop."

He smiled in gratitude. "Thanks."

She went into the front hall to get it, and carried it back to the family room. Kurt was standing in front of the buggy, looking tenderly at the three baby girls.

Not really surprised he had the potential to be a good father—Kurt was a McCabe, after all—Paige unzipped the leather case. "Where do you want to set up?" she asked casually.

"Sofa's fine." Kurt took one last loving look at the babies and ambled toward her.

Paige unstrapped the laptop from the protective cushion and handed it to him, then reached into the zippered compartment to get the power cord. As it came out, the end of it caught on a pink-and-blue folder. Paige tried to catch it, failed. The folder upended and papers scattered across the coffee table and onto the floor, including the contract she had recently signed.

She flushed and made a panicked grab for it. Fortunately, Kurt was so involved in powering up her computer that she was able to collect everything before he saw what it was.

As coolly as possible, she stuffed the papers back into the partitioned divider within the case. Then turned to find him waiting to hand the laptop back to her. "You want to log on?"

She nodded. And thanks to the Triple Diamond Ranch Wi-Fi, quickly got online. She passed it back again. "All yours."

Kurt typed in a few commands and brought up his webmail. "Anything?" Paige asked as the babies began to stir. She walked over to gently jiggle the buggy with a soothing back-and-forth motion. To her relief, the infants settled right back down.

"Nope. I'll email her, though." He paused thoughtfully. "Sometimes when Camila is working she turns off her phones."

Nerves jangling, Paige continued to pace the room. "Does she text-message?"

"Not if she's turned off her phone. But she always checks her email at some point during the day."

Paige couldn't help but note that Kurt typed with the same masculine efficiency he used for everything else. "What are you going to say?"

He treated her to a careless smile and waggled his dark brows. "Nosey, aren't you?"

Paige rolled her eyes. The man could not stop dragging her back to their teenage one-upmanship, and the welter of complex emotions it always brought forth. She peered down her nose at him. "You might say I have a vested interest in this situation being resolved as quickly as possible. And you didn't answer my question."

Laconically, he turned the laptop so she could see the screen.

Paige paced close enough to read aloud, "'Camila, I

need to see you. It's important. Kurt.' That's all you're going to say?"

"It's all I need to say." He clicked on Send.

Men! Especially those of few words and contained emotions! Frustrated that he didn't seem to be taking his pursuit of his ex half as seriously as he was taking his current pursuit of her, Paige warned, "Camila's going to want to know what it's about."

Kurt leaned back against the sofa and stretched his arms above his head. "If she left the triplets here, she will know."

"But if she didn't leave them..."

His lips thinned. "She must have. Otherwise where did they come from?"

"You're asking me."

Kurt clamped his arms over his rock-solid chest. "Obviously. Not."

The laptop dinged.

"Aha!" He checked the in-box. "I knew it! She answered."

Paige wished Kurt had thought to do this hours ago. Curious, she asked, "What did she say?"

"She italicized *I need to see you* and then wrote 'Like that is going to happen.'" Kurt grimaced and swore. Lips set, he typed again.

"What are you saying this time?"

Kurt quoted from the screen, "'Camila, do you know anything about the triplets?'"

"Well, that's a little better."

"Thank you, Coach."

"I just meant..."

"I know what you meant. What I need to figure out is what Camila is thinking and feeling right now."

Paige needed to discern that, too.

A tense minute passed. Then another. Finally, the new-message ding sounded. Making no effort to disguise her insatiable need to know, Paige leaned over his shoulder and read Camila's response.

They're your brothers, Kurt. Not mine! Now stop calling me and emailing me and leave me alone! Signing off...indefinitely...Camila

Paige furrowed her brow. "Wrong set of triplets."

"No kidding." Kurt swore once again.

"Is she messing with you. Or...?"

Still staring at the screen, he frowned. "I have no clue. What I do know," he concluded tensely, "is that's it. I'm not going to hear anything more from Camila tonight. And maybe not tomorrow, either." He switched off the laptop and slid it back in the case. "When Camila gets ticked off, she goes into her 'cave' and doesn't come out until she's good and ready."

"What kind of relationship did you have? I mean, I know you dated for a long time." A surprisingly long time...

He zipped the case shut and rose from the sofa. "Five years, on and off."

Paige tamped down a wave of unexpected jealousy. "How serious were you?"

"Not serious at all." Kurt walked over to the fireplace and studied the dwindling flames. "That was the agreement. She wasn't interested in marriage any more than I was. We were both too focused on our careers. Plus—" he bent to remove the screen "—with the way Camila works..."

Paige sauntered closer. "I know when she's writing a screenplay she holes up in a hotel until it's done, and has very little contact with anyone. My parents have talked about that."

Kurt added another log to the fire. "And when she's not writing something new, she's usually involved in rewrites."

"Which means she's on a movie set," Paige said.

"Right." He poked at the logs until they were arranged the way he wanted. He replaced the screen and set the poker back in the stand. "Which means she could be anywhere in the world. So when we were officially an item, sometimes we would see each other every day for two weeks, and then we might not see each other at all for four months. Then we'd be together for two days, and spend another month apart. You get the idea."

A feeling of discontent sifted through Paige. "And you were okay with that."

"Yeah," he replied. "Casual relationships don't get much better than that."

Paige edged closer, wanting to understand. "So what happened?" she asked softly.

His lips twisted pensively. "Camila had her thirty-second birthday and suddenly wanted to get married. She didn't want anything else to change, just wanted a ring on her finger."

It wasn't hard to see how that had gone over. "And you balked."

Regret mingled with the confusion in his expression.

"I didn't see the point. If you're going to be married you need to commit to living together at least most of the time."

On that, Paige agreed. Marriage required commitment, and both of those things demanded sacrifice and compromise. Otherwise, as Kurt said, what was the point? "And Camila wouldn't do that."

"No." The word was rife with bitterness.

And everything else he wasn't saying.

"Did you ask her to give up her work?" Paige asked.

He gave her a steady look that sent heat spiraling through her. "I would no more do that than offer to give up mine. Being a writer is as much who she is as being a doctor is who you are. Just as being a vet is who I am. Anyway, she ended it and stopped speaking to me."

And that, apparently, was that. "So you're not carrying a torch," Paige noted.

"No. And I don't think she is, either, judging from her response just now."

Which meant *what,* regarding the babies? Paige wondered. Camila didn't want them any more than she wanted Kurt? "So what now?" she asked impatiently.

Kurt glanced at the buggy, where the babies still slept peacefully. "We fix another round of bottles, get ready for the next feeding, and we wait."

"YOU TWO LOOK TERRIBLE," Kyle noted when he showed up at seven the next morning, bakery box in hand.

Paige grinned at Kurt's twin brother and replied drolly, "Thanks."

"Seriously." Kyle looked at Lindsay, who was in

Paige's arms, and Lori and Lucille, who were cradled in Kurt's. "How bad was the night?"

"Depends on what you mean by bad," Kurt said.

Unshaved, dark hair askew, his clothing rumpled and stained with spit-up, he looked as if he'd experienced an all-nighter from hell. Paige knew she was equally disheveled. "If you mean were we short on sleep," she told Kyle, "the answer is yes."

Freshly shaved and showered, and in casual clothing, Kurt's brother studied the triplets. "Looks like they're getting sleepy now."

"Don't rub it in," she moaned.

"So they haven't slept since yesterday?"

Kurt shook his head. "They slept all evening. When we were awake."

"Correct me if I'm wrong," Kyle said, walking over to power on the single brew coffeemaker on the counter, "but aren't new parents—which is sort of what you are here, temporarily anyway—supposed to sleep whenever the baby sleeps?"

Paige used her free hand to open the bakery box. Inside was the most luscious array of freshly baked doughnuts she had ever seen. "That is the usual plan. And these look delicious, Kyle."

"Glad you think so. Help yourself. I figured as long as I was going to have to endure all the 'deputy' jokes from my brother here, I might as well bring the doughnuts along."

"Good thing you did." Finding she was starving, Paige plucked a vanilla-pecan doughnut from the box.

Kyle walked over to relieve Kurt of one of the triplets. Lucille looked at Kurt, then Kyle, as if trying to figure out how "daddy" had suddenly turned into a before-and-after simulation. Stymied, too tired to care, she rested her head on Kyle's shoulder.

"Thanks for everything but the insult," Kurt told his twin.

"No problem." Kyle cuddled Lucille with the same gentle strength and tender fascination all McCabes evidenced. "There are plenty more smart remarks where that came from."

Kurt rolled his eyes at the teasing, took a chocolate doughnut from the box, scarfed it down in three bites and helped himself to another. "So what's going on with the investigation?" he asked.

"Not much. There are still no reports on missing or abandoned children, or a mother acting erratically."

"What about checking the birth records, seeing if the kids are Camila's babies and if I am already listed as their legal father?" Kurt asked, impatient to get the situation squared away and to verify that the children were indeed his.

Kyle shook his head. "We can't do that without Camila's permission, or having some proof that you are the triplets' biological father. That would be a HIPAA violation."

Holding the baby in one arm, and eating with her other hand, Paige explained, "Although they used to be part of the public domain, medical privacy laws keep all birth and death records confidential now."

"But that doesn't mean we can't start an active police investigation," Kyle said, understanding his twin's desperation to get the truth. "Given what we have to go on now, the fact they were left with you, I'm going to assume the babies were born somewhere in Texas, and check with the state Bureau of Vital Statistics in Austin, first thing Monday morning."

"Why not now?" Kurt pressed.

Kyle shrugged while Paige finished downing her breakfast. "It's the weekend," he reminded him. "Their offices are closed until Monday."

Kurt's frustration grew. He was used to getting things done quickly and efficiently. This seemed like a bureaucratic nightmare. "There's nothing we can do until then? No one to call in an emergency?" And for him, this was an emergency.

Paige walked to the sink to rinse off her free hand. "Ten or fifteen years ago, we could have contacted all the hospitals and doctors in the area directly. We can't do that now without first obtaining a court order." Finished, she blotted her hand on a dish towel.

Kyle nodded. "And we can't get a court order to go searching through tons of privileged medical records without first demonstrating that all other avenues did not reveal the information." He sighed. "So like it or not, it's the state Bureau of Vital Statistics first. Hopefully, the girls' births will have been registered—since that is supposed to be done within thirty days—and we're well past that. If all goes smoothly, we'll get the information rather quickly on Monday and can go from there."

"And if they aren't registered?" Kurt asked.

"Then we'll find another way," his brother assured him.

"I guess it won't be that hard, given the fact that they are triplets." Kurt exhaled. "I mean, how often does that happen?"

"Approximately two thousand times a year in the United States," Paige said. Both men turned to look at her in surprise. She shrugged. "I'm a pediatrician. I know those statistics."

"Roughly how many sets of triplets are born in Texas?"

The picture of maternal bliss, Paige cuddled Lindsay tenderly. "Anywhere from fifty to one hundred annually. It varies widely."

"That still helps us narrow the search considerably," Kyle said. "Especially if—as we all assume—the names on those gold ID bracelets are the kids' correct monikers."

He had a point there, Kurt thought. How many sets of identical female triplets could have been born in the last three months or so, bearing the names Lori, Lucille and Lindsay? He began to feel more confident this would be resolved quickly. "So what next?"

"I've put out an alert to other police officials throughout the nation, asking to be notified if there are any reports of missing multiples. So far, nothing's showed up." Kyle paused. "But…if we get desperate for leads, down the road we can always hold a press conference and see what we can get that way."

Most likely lots of false leads, Kurt thought. And wild speculation and constant interference from the tabloid press.

Paige helped Lindsay work up a burp. "The resulting media circus probably wouldn't be good for the kids. And it might scare away or further upset the mother."

Which was something none of them wanted, Kurt thought. He met Paige's eyes, surprised to find them once again on the exact same wavelength. "I agree. We do that only as a last resort." Hopefully, it wouldn't come to that.

He rubbed a hand across the tense muscles in the back of his neck. "Although this could just be a misguided attempt to teach me some sort of lesson," he theorized aloud, "it could also be a sign that their mother—or Camila—is simply too overwhelmed at the moment to think straight or cope with the demands of three infants."

"She could very well be suffering from exhaustion and postpartum depression. After last night, I can certainly understand how that would happen," Paige murmured, swaying back and forth as the baby in her arms got sleepier and sleepier. "And there were two of us here, Kurt. I can't imagine how a single parent could manage on her own. Not without plenty of outside help."

He concurred with that. He'd had plenty of experience caring for nieces and nephews—albeit ones a bit older than this. Paige was a pediatrician, and hence no stranger to infants or sleepless nights, either. And yet she had still felt as overwhelmed at times as he had caring for the babies through the night.

Kyle walked over and slid a premeasured container of coffee into the instant brewer. He turned back to Paige and Kurt. "Look, I know this is frustrating for you, but we will get it worked out eventually, one way or another. It's just going to take a little time." He gazed down at the baby in his arms. "In the meantime, I'm off today. I can hang around for a bit and help out before I head to the station to continue hunting for information." He glanced at Paige, affable as ever. "So if you want to catch forty winks…"

Without warning, Kurt imagined how Paige would look in some sort of silky negligee, snuggled in bed, her lips soft and bare, her auburn hair fanning across her pillow. Irritated, he pushed the tantalizing image away. It was no time to be thinking about how lovely she was, and sure as hell not the time to be considering putting the moves on her. Chances were, when this weekend was over they'd go back to their previous rancor and avoidance strategy.

Oblivious to the conflicted nature of his thoughts, Paige said wistfully, "I'd really love a long hot shower if you're sure you don't mind."

"Not at all," the detective offered gallantly.

The image of Paige sudsing up beneath the hot, steamy spray was even more disturbing. Eager to erase that from his mind, and get them back to the safety zone of their former animosity, Kurt closed the distance between them. He used his free hand to ruffle her hair the way a fifth-grader messes up the hair of a girl he has a crush on, and was rewarded with an irked glare, before he relieved her of her young charge.

"Seriously," he told her as he settled the sleeping Lindsay back in the buggy. "Get a little shut-eye, too, if you want. We men are fine."

Paige scowled. "In case you've forgotten, cowboy, I'm a doctor. I'm used to going without sleep, too!"

Kurt chuckled, pleased to have gotten under her skin again, and watched as she headed off without a backward glance.

KURT AND KYLE WERE RIGHT, Paige thought. A time-out was just what she needed. If she didn't get her perspective back, she would start falling in love with the three baby girls. And she couldn't allow herself to do that, any more than she could let her physical attraction to Kurt take flight. It wasn't just that he was an incredibly sexy man, and a very good kisser. Or the fact that she clearly had been without sexual companionship for far too long, and was hence vulnerable in that regard.

Taking care of the triplets last night had given her and Kurt a false sense of camaraderie. She'd allowed that, plus her desire for a baby of her own, to fuel the real-life fantasy. She'd let herself be swept up in the romance of the situation. And while the intellectual side of her knew Kurt's kiss had been nothing more than an emotional reaction to that, her body still remembered all too well what it had felt like to be held in his arms, to have him kiss her—and to kiss him in return.

If it was just the two of them…

If the babies belonged only to Kurt…

Maybe then she could let her feelings run wild for just a little while and enjoy the bliss of caring for the triplets a little longer.

But there was a woman out there somewhere, waiting in the wings, Paige reminded herself sternly. A woman who might very well want Kurt back in her life. And if that was the case, well, Paige knew how the McCabe men were. They valued duty and honor. They married the mother of their children, no question. So…she needed to be smart here. Forget how good it had felt to be held in Kurt's arms. And look out for herself and her own needs, as well as those of the three baby girls.

Happily, the shower and shampoo were as heavenly as she expected them to be. Feeling simultaneously invigorated and relaxed, Paige stepped out of the stall and wrapped herself in her robe. She put a towel around her hair, to catch the droplets, and went into the bedroom.

She'd laid her clothes out on the bed. Too tired to put them on that second, she stretched out and rested her head on the pillow for just a second.

The next thing she knew she was starting to wake. She sat up quickly, the blood rushing to her head. Looking at her watch, she saw that four hours had passed!

Embarrassed, she quickly dressed and stepped into her boots.

When she pulled the towel off her hair, she saw the auburn strands had dried in unruly waves and kinks. Unfortunately, she had forgotten to bring her hair straightener, so she brushed it and let it go. Paige hastily applied makeup and a dab of perfume, then went to join the twins. And found Kurt stretched out in a recliner, a baby in each arm. All three were snoring gently.

Kyle was seated on the sofa, a slumbering triplet held against his chest. The only one awake, he was contentedly watching college football. "Hey," he whispered, smiling when he saw her.

Wondering why Kurt couldn't treat her with the polite civility of his twin brother, Paige ambled closer. "I'm so sorry," she whispered back. "I fell asleep."

He grinned and pointed. "So did he."

"How long have the triplets been sleeping?" Being careful not to touch Kurt, she lifted Lucille off his broad chest and gently transferred her to the buggy.

"Since a minute after you left."

Paige removed Lindsay in turn and settled her next to her sister. "Of course."

"Kurt sacked out then, too." Kyle stood and handed Lori to Paige. "I'm going to head off. But before I do, I've got some stuff in my pickup truck for you. Hang on while I go get it."

KURT WOKE TO THE SOUND OF soft voices and the front door opening and shutting. For a moment he was disoriented. Where were the two infants he'd had sleeping on his chest? Then he looked over and saw the buggy, where all three were once again sleeping side by side.

He frowned and looked at his watch. He couldn't believe that it was nearly one o'clock in the afternoon. Before he could clear his head, Paige strolled in. She looked amazing with her autumn hair tumbling wildly to her shoulders. He admired the soft white sweater, similar in style to the one she'd had on yesterday, dark blue jeans and boots that she'd changed into. Wow, that woman sure cleaned up well...

"You're awake," she said.

He ran a hand over his face and encountered the stubble of beard. "Yeah." Barely. "Where's Kyle?"

Appearing rested and—unlike him—wide-awake, Paige explained with customary attention to detail, "He went on to the station. He brought us three infant seats from your sibs, in case we get cabin fever and want to go anywhere. He installed the bases for them in the back seat of my station wagon for me before he left—the handled carriers that double as infant seats and snap into them are in the front hall." She took a breath. "He also said to tell you that the triplets—Teddy, Trevor and

Tyler—and their wives will all be dropping by to see you and the kids at some point over the weekend."

Kurt wasn't surprised—his three older brothers were always around to help when trouble came calling, and even when it didn't. "How'd they hear about this?"

Paige chewed on her lower lip. "Apparently, everyone in town knows." Her green eyes shimmered with a mixture of concern and regret. "The only reason we haven't been deluged with visitors thus far is that your parents put the word out for everyone to stay away, lest the triplets' mother try and return, and be scared off by all the perceived activity."

Silence fell between them. Figuring as a pediatrician she was bound to have more experience in situations like this, Kurt asked eventually, "Do you think Camila will come back to claim them before the weekend is up?"

"I don't know." Paige met his searching gaze. "What do you think?"

He exhaled in frustration. "I don't know, either."

The only thing Kurt did know for certain was that he was beginning to depend on Paige to help him manage the situation. And that couldn't be good—for either of them.

Chapter Five

"How long do you think the little darlin's are going to sleep this time?" Kurt asked Paige four hours, two diaper changes and two bottles apiece later.

Feeling as if she had just run a marathon, Paige settled the last infant into the buggy and tucked the blanket around her. "I have no idea," she murmured. "As far as I can tell, the girls aren't on any particular schedule. But their wakefulness could just be due to the fact that they're in a different environment."

"And miss their mom."

"Maybe," Paige allowed. Although to her surprise the girls weren't crying the way kids did when they had bonded to only one person, and were suddenly without that person. The three of them seemed okay with strangers. Which made her wonder all over again what kind of situation they had exited. They seemed well cared for. Loved. And loving in return.

Kurt glanced at her. "Did you ever have lunch?" he asked.

Now that he mentioned it... "Uh...no," Paige replied, surprised to suddenly be the recipient of the gallantry he worked so hard to hide. Unable to deny how handsome and relaxed he looked in a domestic setting, she regarded him curiously. "Did *you* ever get anything besides doughnuts to eat today?"

"No." He rubbed his taut belly longingly. "And I'm famished. I was thinking about running into town and picking up some dinner for us."

Paige grimaced. "That would take at least an hour. Half an hour drive there, half an hour back." As the day had worn on, the weather had taken on a typical November gloom. It was barely five o'clock and already nearly dark. A cold rain fell, drenching the ground and adding the kind of damp chill that was difficult to shake off. "Plus it's Saturday night and all the restaurants are bound to be very busy, with delays for take-out orders." Which would add even more time. "Why don't I just fix us something to eat?"

Paige headed for the kitchen and opened Annie and Travis McCabe's well-stocked fridge. "Eggs?"

It was Kurt's turn to make a face. He shook his head, no doubt recalling their cold cereal-and-fruit dinner the evening before. "I'm going to need something a lot more substantial than that."

She eyed his six-five frame, thinking about how much food it would take to fuel his well-muscled physique. "How about chicken-fried steak with cream gravy then?"

He grinned.

Bingo! "Mashed potatoes," Paige added. Luckily for her, Annie McCabe had stocked the already prepared kind, which only required reheating in the microwave. Ditto for the freezer vegetables. "And green beans."

"Sounds great." His blue eyes narrowed. "But…can you make that?"

His skepticism ignited the rivalry from years past. "Can I make that!" Paige retorted, determined to show off now that she had the chance. "C'mon! I grew up on a ranch!"

He shrugged his broad shoulders. "So did I." The corners of his chiseled lips tugged upward. "But I don't know how to cook chicken-fried steak."

Paige smiled, glad she once again had something to do besides notice how good Kurt looked, freshly showered and shaved, as if ready for a casual Saturday night date. Pulse racing, she turned away from him. "Fortunately for you, I do. It's one of the first dishes my dad taught me how to cook."

Kurt lounged against the counter, the picture of lazy male satisfaction. "What about your mom?"

Paige turned her eyes from the crisply ironed navy blue shirt that brought out the blue of his eyes. She did not need to be noticing how well the cotton clung to his nicely muscled pecs and abs. Never mind how well his worn jeans gloved the most masculine part of him. "Mom's the baker in the family. My dad is the one who cooks the down-home Texas cuisine."

"Well, okay then."

Kurt grinned at her, then segued into the helpfulness she found far too compelling. "What can I do?"

Stop looking at me as if you're suddenly wanting to kiss me again, as much as I'd like to kiss you….

For both their sakes, Paige forced herself to put on her emotional armor once again. "Could you build a fire, please? It's kind of chilly in here." She didn't want any excuses to end up in his arms. She was way too aware of Kurt as it was.

"Will do."

He strode toward the front hall. The door closed after him, and Paige got to work, defrosting the round steak. By the time he came back in, she'd gotten the glass canister of flour out of the pantry, the spices she needed from the rack next to the stove, and had beaten the eggs and milk together.

While the babies slept and Kurt built the fire, she tenderized the steak with a mallet and prepared three dishes, two of flour and one with the egg-and-milk mixture.

Kurt strolled back in as she seasoned the meat and then set the first piece of steak in the flour. She coated it, then turned it over on the other side and coated that, too. Or tried to—for some reason the flour wasn't sticking to the thick slab of tenderized beefsteak.

Paige tried again, frowning as the flour seemed to disappear into the meat, then set the slab of steak in the egg-and-milk mixture, and from there back into the second plate of flour. Again, she had the same problem. The flour kept disappearing into the egg-and-milk coating the beef, instead of forming a crust on the outside, as it should have.

"Something wrong?" Kurt asked.

Embarrassed to have already hit a snag in the meal prep, when she had just bragged to her former rival about her prowess in the kitchen, Paige pretended an ease she couldn't begin to feel. "Um, no," she murmured, determined not to fall apart, no matter how tired and out of her element she was. "I was just... Do you think you could check the weather for me?" She pointed upward. "I'm a little concerned about that rain drumming on the roof."

Kurt's eyes reflected his surprise. "Sure. I don't think it's anything to worry about, though. It's still well above freezing."

Paige nodded and surreptitiously turned her attention back to what she was doing. The darn flour still wasn't sticking! Even after the meat had gone into the egg-milk bath, and back into the flour again! Not wanting Kurt to notice how much difficulty she was having with something so basic and simple, she lifted her shoulder in a coquettish shrug. Worked what feminine wiles she possessed to distract him from what was really going on—a culinary disaster in the making. "Even so..." she said stubbornly.

Kurt continued to watch her curiously. He knew something was going on with her; he just didn't know what. But that wasn't unusual, either. The two of them had never really understood one another. "Sure," he drawled finally, then sauntered off, whistling.

Flushing at her sudden ineptness as a chef, Paige went over to check the skillet, found it ready. She dropped the meat into the sizzling oil. Then went back to try the second steak, figuring she would eat the first, and give him the second.

Unfortunately, the second slab was no more cooperative. She did the best she could, pressing the flour into the meat with the back of a spoon, over and over, until enough of a coating stuck that it was covered in white, then transferred it to the sizzling pan.

Kurt came back in. "It's supposed to rain until

morning, but only an inch is predicted, so we should be fine. There's no danger of ice or flooding."

Paige ducked her head so she didn't have to meet his gaze and risk him seeing the failure and frustration in her eyes. "Good."

"You sure you're feeling okay?" He surveyed her with a puzzled frown and a steady, assessing look. "Your cheeks are a little pink," he noted in obvious concern.

With embarrassment, Paige thought. She still couldn't figure out what was going on with her chicken-fried steak. The breading was now sticking to the meat, and browning, but the crust didn't look the way it normally did. And the remaining oil in the skillet was thickening, even before she added the flour to make the roux. It smelled a little off, too.

Not bad, exactly, just *different...*

Eager to distract Kurt, she murmured, "If you want to set the table and make some coffee, I'll nuke the green beans and the mashed potatoes."

He flashed an agreeable smile. "No problem."

As he got busy, Paige removed the fork-tender steaks from the skillet and put them on a platter. She added a little flour to the thickly bubbling oil in the bottom of the pan, stirred it into a roux, and then added cream, salt and pepper, and continued to stir until it achieved the consistency of a thick white gravy.

While that was going on, she cooked the vegetables in the microwave, then plated both meals, using a generous slathering of cream gravy to hide each steak's funky looking crust.

Kurt smiled as she brought their dinners to the kitchen table. "This is really great, thanks."

What was it her mother always said? The way to a man's heart was through his stomach? Although that was definitely not the intent here, Paige told herself firmly. She was simply trying to do the sensible thing and feed them, rather than force him to go out. "No problem." She sat across from him and picked up her fork, almost afraid to taste the meat.

Paige's fear increased when she saw the look on Kurt's face when the first bite of steak hit his tongue. There *was* something wrong! Panic returned, big-time. "What?" she demanded.

The surprise in Kurt's eyes faded. His expression turned politely inscrutable. "Nothing. It's great."

Who was he kidding?

But knowing he wasn't going to tell her what the problem was, whatever it was, Paige took a bite. And nearly gagged at the strangely sweet, sort of icky taste. What the heck…? It was all she could do to swallow! "Oh my goodness, that's awful!"

"No…" He waved off her concern, still ready to take one for the team. The only problem was, she didn't want him to sacrifice for her this way. Paige pushed back from the table and gulped water to get rid of the taste. "Don't lie to me. It's terrible!" She stared at her plate, trying to figure out what had gone wrong. "I don't understand. Why does that taste so weird?" She looked at him, wondering if he had the answer.

Kurt shrugged. Apparently reluctant to wound her, he finally lifted his brow and ventured cautiously, "Is it steak? I mean, you didn't cook liver or something, did you?"

The heat in her cheeks deepened. "No." Feeling both

exasperated and humiliated, Paige got up and went to the trash and fished out the wrapper. "See? It says right here!" She pointed in aggravation. "Round steak!"

"Then...?" Kurt seemed as puzzled as she felt.

Paige rubbed at the tension in her temples. "There was nothing wrong with the egg or the milk. They were both fresh."

He shook his head stoically. "It doesn't matter—we can still eat it. It's fine," he said, forking up another bite.

Paige snorted. Fine her foot! With the thoroughness she had once used in chem lab, she continued going over the specifics. "The only seasonings I used were salt and pepper. So the only thing left is the—" her body sagged as the next thought hit "—flour," she finished weakly.

Kurt blinked. "What?"

Beginning to suspect what may have happened, Paige rushed over to open the clear plastic canister she had used. She took a long hard look, then dipped a spoon in, removed a small portion and lifted it to her nose.

"Is the *flour* bad?" he asked in concern.

She grimaced, every ounce of pride she had drained out of her. Reluctantly, she turned her gaze to him. "I wouldn't know. Because this isn't flour, Kurt," she admitted. "It's confectioner's sugar."

KURT STARED AT HER as if unable to comprehend what she was saying. Then a laugh erupted from deep within him. He chuckled till he cried, then laughed some more, while Paige buried her face in her hands, feeling as if she were going to die of embarrassment. Of all the times to screw up…the first time she made a meal for him was definitely not it!

He got up and came to her side. "Hey." All warmth and compassion now, he put both his arms around her. And when she still wouldn't look at him, he tucked a hand beneath her chin. "It could have happened to anyone," he soothed.

Really? "Nice try."

"We can still eat it. Just pretend it's kind of a fusion, down-home Texas and Asian dish. If you're expecting it to be sweet, it's going to taste good." He took her hand and led her back to the table. "Trust me."

Paige rolled her eyes and sat down. Inhaling deeply, she took another bite. "It's still awful."

"It's good," he insisted, even more passionately. "It was made with love."

The word startled both of them. It was his turn to flush slightly and look uncomfortable. "You know what I mean." Kurt glossed over his use of the word. "Your heart was in the right place. It was a great effort," he stated firmly.

Paige rolled her eyes. She did not welcome his pity now any more than she had his fierce competitive attitude in days gone by. She glared at him and sat back, tapping her fork against her plate. "That sounds like a locker-room speech for losers."

Her grumbling only amused him further. "You're funny."

Lamenting the waste of perfectly good beefsteak, Paige sighed. "I wish this meal was." She ate her green beans and mashed potatoes, while Kurt chowed down on the entire plate, as if it was just what he had been waiting for.

She had to admire his gusto. Even if she couldn't quite bring herself to act so courageously.

He regarded her curiously. "I take it this has never happened to you before."

"No." Paige pushed her plate aside and rested her elbows on the table. She pressed her fingertips to her temples. "I mean, of course I've screwed up in the kitchen—everybody does from time to time—but it's usually too much salt in something, or an ingredient I forgot. Something slight that is easily remedied."

"Well, think of the story you'll have to tell your kids."

"And yours," Paige replied flippantly. *Or ours.*

Whoa! Where had thought come from?

She really was tired. Probably too tired to be spending time alone with him. She stood and carried her dish to the sink.

He brought over his empty plate.

Their shoulders bumped as they bent to put their dishes in the dishwasher.

Paige drew back. Their gazes locked, and she realized that Kurt really had grown up, same as she. Not bothering to hide her admiration, she said, "Thanks for being a good sport."

He nodded, as if that had been the only path to take. "Thanks for making dinner."

Silence fell between them once again. Apparently noting the tense, uneasy set of her shoulders, he reached over and tucked her hair behind her ear. "This wasn't a big deal," he repeated.

Paige sighed as her next worry hit. "But it could have been," she murmured.

He raised a brow. "What do you mean?"

Reminded how very much was at stake here, Paige turned her glance away. "I'm a pediatric surgeon, Kurt. There's no room in my life for mistakes."

He put his hands on her shoulders. "This wasn't an operating room."

She ignored the comforting warmth radiating from his palms. "Suppose it had been?"

"Whoa."

She pulled away and threaded her hands through her hair. "I'm so tired I can barely think." *Plus, I wanted to impress you. And really, how stupid was that?* Shaking her head, she began to pace. "I'm used to excelling. I should be able to do it all. Juggle home and kids and work and everything else I need to juggle. Instead, after twenty-four hours as a foster mom, I'm a colossal failure."

He caught up with her. "You're exaggerating."

Paige spun around, refusing to be mollified. "Am I? I'm the one who thought the kids would sleep last night if we kept them up in the evening. Instead, they were up all night, slept all morning and then were up all afternoon. And now they're asleep again!" What she had managed to accomplish was so far from what she advised her patients' parents to do it was almost laughable.

Kurt shrugged and leaned in close. "So maybe we should do what all new parents do, and sleep while we can."

Paige's heart took on a slow, heavy beat. "What are you saying?"

He looked confident as he closed the distance between them. "That everything you're feeling can be fixed with one thing. Sleep!"

Paige wasn't quite sure how it happened. One minute she was standing there arguing with him—and the next, he'd swung her up off her feet and was holding her against his broad chest. "What in the world do you think you are doing?" she demanded.

"Putting you to bed for a nap."

She fought the unexpected thrill coursing through her, and struggled to get a handle on her soaring emotions. "You can't do that!"

He flashed a tantalizing half smile and carried her down the hall. "Au contraire, it appears that I am, Dr. Chamberlain."

"Seriously, Kurt…" She could feel his body heat, and breathed in the enticing wintry fragrance of his cologne.

"Seriously." He set her down next to her bed and took her face in his hands, but refrained from kissing her again. Instead, his gaze lingered on her lips. "I'll take the first watch while you get some rest."

Her heart kicking against her ribs, Paige watched in frustration as he turned and left.

PAIGE THOUGHT ABOUT GOING to sleep. With her heart all aflutter and her libido in overdrive, she knew it was not going to happen. That didn't mean she couldn't use the time to good advantage, however. Determined to get the situation back under control, she grabbed her cell phone and dialed the social worker in charge. "Any new information on the triplets?" she asked.

"Not so far," Mitzy Martin replied with the candor of an old and trusted friend. "I just talked to Kyle—he's not having any luck through police channels, either. But not to worry. We'll come up with a solution for this situation by Monday morning, and you'll be free to go back to your normal life."

For reasons Paige chose not to examine closely, she wasn't as happy to hear that as she thought she should be.

"How are things going with the babies?" Mitzy asked.

Paige thought of the strides they had made in the last twenty-six hours. "Good."

"Kurt?"

Another wave of unexpected anxiety hit, not all of it related to the kids. "He seems to be getting attached." To the triplets, anyway...

"Well, that's good," Mitzy said, "if they are his kids."

But what if they weren't? Paige wondered. What if someone had left the babies with Kurt simply because they wanted the children to have access to the McCabe wealth and clout?

Mitzy continued. "The girls will have a place to go, even if the mother no longer wants to be involved."

And if the mother did want to be involved? What then? Would she be able to emotionally detach herself as swiftly and completely as the situation warranted? Paige sighed. It was hard to believe she herself had gotten so emotionally involved so fast. Was it just because Lindsay, Lori and Lucille were so adorable? Because she wanted children of her own so badly? A part of her wondered if perhaps there was something more behind her riptide of feelings....

"What about you?" Mitzy continued. "Are you still planning to go through with the appointment at the fertility clinic in Dallas Thanksgiving weekend?"

Uncertainty added to Paige's atypically low mood. She frowned. "I think so."

"What do you mean *think* so?" Mitzy repeated, sounding shocked.

Briefly, Paige brought her up to date on the evening's culinary disaster.

"Kurt is right. That could've happened to anyone," Mitzy said firmly. "One semi-ruined dinner doesn't mean you won't be a good mom, when the time comes. In addition to the fact you will only have one infant to contend with—unless you *want* more than that at a time—"

"Uh, no," Paige said quickly. The weekend had shown her that would be too hard for any single parent. Which was no doubt part—or even all—of the reason the babies had ended up on the McCabes' doorstep. They knew how to bring up twins and triplets....

Oblivious to Paige's thoughts, Mitzy continued her pep talk. "In the future, you will have your parents' help. And plenty of time to arrange for a full-time, live-in nanny slash housekeeper, so it's not going to be nearly as challenging as this weekend. Hence, you will be a great mom, all on your own, and you'll continue to be a great doctor. Have you picked out a daddy yet?"

She hesitated. "I haven't really had time to go through the profiles."

"Well, you better get to it," Mitzy advised, cheerful

as ever. "As long as you get to choose, you might as well select carefully! In the meantime, call me if you need me."

"Will do," Paige promised.

The two women hung up. Realizing her best friend was right—she did need to concentrate more on her future family and fixate less on her present alliance with Kurt and the triplets—Paige got the folder out of her briefcase and then climbed back on her bed. It was still raining; she could hear droplets drumming on the roof. She drew the down comforter from the foot of the bed and laid it across her lap. Settled against the pillows, she began going through the profiles. There were no pictures, so she had to go solely by the facts. *Blond hair, blue eyes, six feet tall...athletic...IQ of 130.* Nope. *Auburn hair, green eyes, musically gifted, artistic.* Also no. *Black hair, brown eyes.* Nope. *Dark brown hair, amber eyes.* Also no. Paige flipped through the various profiles, looking to see if any of the potential donors had dark hair and McCabe-blue eyes. Or were six feet five inches tall. Broad shouldered. Incredibly good with animals and children alike.

The answer was no.

Not unless she wanted Kurt McCabe to be the daddy of her child.

Paige smirked at the ludicrous idea and went back to the stack of profiles. She really had to get a grip. Kurt McCabe was not in the running for daddy of her child. And the sooner she got that through her head, the better off they all would be.

Chapter Six

"Paige, wake up!"

The low masculine voice was reverberating in her ear, and Paige opened her eyes to see Kurt bent over her. He looked as ruggedly handsome in person as he had in her dreams, and even more purposeful.

In the distance, she could hear the triplets wailing. Panic shot through her. "What happened?" She bolted upright and a second later her feet hit the floor.

His demeanor tense and concerned, Kurt whirled and headed for the door. "They started waking up about ten minutes ago. I tried feeding Lindsay first, but then Lori and Lucille got impatient, and you can hear what's happening now."

Paige certainly could. It sounded like a mass mutiny! She was fast on Kurt's heels as they reached the family room. All three babies were back in the buggy, with arms flailing, mouths open and tears running down their cute little faces.

Her heart going out to the distraught infants, Paige scooped up Lucille. Kurt lifted Lindsay and then Lori into his arms. The physical comfort and cuddling did nothing. The crying continued full force. In the kitchen, two premade bottles were warming in big bowls of water. The other was set on a table next to the man-size rocker in the family room.

Paige shouted to be heard above the cacophony. "We've got to feed them all at once."

Kurt tried to do so, but the awkward method he used—having a baby in each arm and propping the end of one bottle against his chest and chin—didn't work, since the furious infants kept squirming, flailing and knocking the bottles full of formula away.

"How?" he asked, clearly exasperated.

"We'll sit side by side on the sofa." Paige knelt, and collected the rejected bottles. She carried them to the kitchen and washed the nipples under the tap, then returned to the sofa.

Kurt took the middle cushion, got settled again with a distraught baby in each arm. She helped him position the bottles. Lori and Lucille still refused to eat. Paige sat down next to them and offered the third bottle to the wailing infant she held. But by now Lindsay was too worked up to cooperate, and pushed the nipple away, screaming all the louder. Paige and Kurt tried singing. Still no go.

"Maybe we just need to do this differently," Paige said. She went back to the bedroom and returned, Lindsay in one arm and two pillows in the other. Once again, Paige sat down next to Kurt, but this time propped her feet on the coffee table, knees up, and positioned a pillow across her thighs. She helped Kurt do the same. They then moved the babies so they were lying with their backs against the pillow, heads slightly elevated, tiny feet resting on Paige's and Kurt's tummies.

"Now, let's try this again," Paige told the perplexed but slightly quieter babies. She offered a bottle. Kurt offered two.

Seconds later, the triplets were drinking contentedly, staring at the adults all the while. Kurt grinned and looked over at Paige. "Way to go, *Mom*," he said.

Mom.

The word carried with it a wealth of memories and a heart full of hope. Paige knew Kurt had meant it as a joke. A play on the whole temporary-foster-mom thing. But that playful endearment coming from his lips hit her where she was most vulnerable.

She glanced away and quipped self-effacingly, "I occasionally come up with a good idea or two."

"Well, this was genius," he declared.

Paige wouldn't go that far, although it was nice to hear Kurt say it.

They paused to burp all three babies, then resumed feeding them the rest of their bottles.

The triplets drank quickly. Finally, their appetites were satisfied. Once again, the burps came quickly and easily.

Paige smiled and rose, with Lindsay cradled in her arms. "You know what? Now would be a good time to give them their baths." She knew she was babbling self-consciously, but she couldn't help it. Anything to keep from looking Kurt in the eye, or letting him realize how much this weekend was quickly coming to mean to her.

Paige gulped, her back still turned to him as she swayed back and forth, cuddling Lindsay. "What time is it, anyway?" Aware that he was oddly silent, she glanced at the grandfather clock. "Ten o'clock! Wow. I must have slept a couple of hours...which means so did they."

Wondering what he was doing, she turned to see Kurt settling Lori and Lucille in the buggy, side by side, with the gentleness of an old pro. He came over to her, met her eyes and wordlessly took Lindsay, setting her in the buggy, too. He covered all three with a blanket, and then swung back to Paige.

"I didn't mean to make you uncomfortable by calling you 'Mom.'"

FOR A SECOND, PAIGE FROZE. She took a step closer, looking more beautiful and hesitant than ever before. Her soft lips curved into an aloof smile. "You didn't." She shrugged her slender shoulders carelessly. "I *am* a foster mom."

He watched, unsure how to help, as she gathered up the empty baby bottles and carried them into the kitchen. Admiring the graceful way she moved, he trailed behind her and observed, "A foster mom who is looking into the whole fertility route thing."

She quickly glanced up at him, her expression unreadable. "How did you know that?" she asked, her tongue darting out to wet her lips.

Kurt stuffed his hands in the pockets of his jeans and rocked back on his heels. "I saw the folder when it fell out of your briefcase last night, and the profiles scattered across your lap in the bedroom."

Pink color flushed her high, sculpted cheekbones.

Kurt knew he was treading in dangerous territory. He lifted a palm. "I know that it's none of my business."

She busied herself, washing the bottles out by hand. Her silky auburn curls fell across her face. "You're right." The corners of her lips turned downward. "It isn't."

He grabbed a dish towel and dried everything she cleaned, aware once again how they were working like a well-oiled team. "But is that really what you want to do?"

She turned toward him, a furrow formed along the bridge of her nose. "I want a baby, Kurt."

Ignoring the pressure at the front of his jeans, he held her steady gaze. "But not a man."

She lounged against the sink, hands clasped around the counter edge on either side of her. Her white cashmere sweater lovingly molded to her breasts, while the sleek denim of her jeans hugged her hips. "I'm not against having a man in my life," she said in a way that dared him to prove otherwise. "Any more than I presume you're against having a woman."

"Then?"

Paige strode back into the family room and checked on the babies. All were fast asleep. Again.

She pivoted away from the sleeping crew, her sock-clad feet moving soundlessly over the carpeted floor. She paced to the wall of windows that overlooked the backyard, and gazed out into the dark, starry night. The rain had stopped, but a wind had whipped up as the cold front that had been expected moved in.

Paige knotted her hands together in front of her. "I haven't found anyone I want to marry. And I'm tired of waiting." She exhaled wistfully, then turned. "And then there's my biological clock. I'm thirty-four." She tensed visibly, on guard once more. "I'm afraid that if I don't get pregnant soon, Mother Nature will intervene and I won't physically be able to have a baby. And to go through life without ever experiencing the wonder of birth…"

Her green eyes glinted with the hurt of her previous miscarriage. "When I know full well that is still within my reach and something I can control…at least to a point…" She drew a deep breath and came closer still. "I have to do this, Kurt. I want to do this."

"So you're going to a sperm bank."

As he'd expected, his taunt raised her hackles.

"It makes sense to me." Paige studied him, obviously not happy about his lack of enthusiasm for her plan. "But not to you," she ventured.

Kurt felt she deserved much more than she was apparently willing to settle for. He looked at her with a challenging smile. "It's not up to me…. I don't have a say in this."

"But if you did?" she pressed, moving closer still.

He inhaled the soft lavender scent of her skin and hair. "I'd say forget the sperm bank. Make a baby with love, the old-fashioned way."

Paige glowed, as if she had been waiting an entire lifetime for that to happen. "Well, in theory, of course that's what I'd want!" she replied, then threw up her hands. "But I can't exactly go up to some guy who has all the characteristics I want and ask him to… C'mon!" She flushed at the unabashedly erotic image her words had evoked—for both of them. Paige swallowed and clamped her arms defiantly in front of her. "You can see how ridiculous that is. Especially when we're talking about the lifelong commitment of a child."

What if they weren't? Kurt wondered. "What if we're talking about a short-term thing?"

"What do you mean?"

He rubbed his jaw in a thoughtful manner. "Would you make love to someone for the sake of making love?" Sliding his palms down her arms, he caught her wrists in his hands and moved them around to the small of her back, so she was arched against him. "Because you want to be physically close?" He let her wrists go, anchored his hands on her waist, then bent and kissed first her temple and then her lips. "Or need comfort that only the warmth of another person's arms can bring?"

Paige opened her mouth to the pressure of his, her defenses beginning to crumble as steadily and surely as his. "I admit sometimes…" she told him breathlessly, between sweet, slow kisses "…like now…" She went up on tiptoe, making a sound that was part whimper of need, part sigh of pure womanly pleasure. He kissed her again, harder now, deeper. "I'm tempted," she admitted, resting her hands on his shoulders. "Very tempted." Her fingers curled warmly over his skin. "But I don't indulge in one-night stands."

He threaded his fingers through her hair and let her know he wanted her desperately, too. "Neither do I."

"So…"

"But right now," Kurt continued, kissing her again, "I think we're treading exactly where we're supposed to be.…"

Paige barely had time to react before his head lowered once again. His mouth joined with hers in a riveting, passionate kiss, and just that suddenly, all thoughts of the future, and her well-considered plans to have a baby the new-fashioned way, fled. She moaned softly as he clasped her to him and deepened the kiss until it was so wild and reckless it buckled her knees and stole her breath. This was how she had always wanted to be kissed, but never had been. He kissed her as if he meant to erase every disappointment she had ever suffered. And she melted against him, savoring the hardness and strength of his chest pressed against her breasts, and lower still, the hardness that brought forth another fierce welter of desire. For too long she had protected her heart, and kept her need for physical closeness, for the sheer pleasure of lovemaking, at bay. *No more,* she thought, as Kurt continued to ravish her with his lips.

"Let me make love to you, Paige," he finally said, breaking the kiss. "Let us be close."

KURT WAITED FOR PAIGE to opt out of this. To let her customary reserve, combined with her distrust of him, prompt her to call a halt to the growing desire welling up between them. "As long as you know it's a one-time-only thing," she murmured.

Kurt didn't want to agree to that stipulation. Not when he already knew that making love to Paige once would never be enough. Not for him, and not for her. But sensing that telling her what she wanted to hear was the only way he would ever get close to her, he nodded his assent. "Unless," he whispered back, lowering his lips to hers once more, "you change your mind. And want to be close like this again."

"I won't," she insisted stubbornly, looking a little apprehensive despite her feisty response.

Yes, Kurt thought, *you will, if I do this right—and I intend to do this right.*

For the second time that evening, he picked Paige up in his arms and carried her to the bedroom. He set her down next to the bed, then went back to get the buggy. He rolled it carefully down the hall, parking it in the room across the hall, then waited to make sure Lindsay, Lori and Lucille were still sound asleep. "So we can hear them if they need us," he explained, going back to Paige.

She'd already picked up the scattered papers, and turned back the covers on her bed. She wreathed her arms about his neck, looked into his eyes. "Let's hope they sleep for a good long while, then," she murmured, the sparkle in her eyes growing ever brighter.

Eager to hold her in his arms, Kurt set his hands on her hips and brought her close once again. He buried first his face and then his hands in her hair. As he tilted her head, he half expected her to stiffen with resistance, given the excessively practical way they were approaching this. Instead, the look in her eyes invited him to run wild with her, and it was an invitation he found as impossible to resist as the soft, womanly feel of her. Slowly, he lowered his lips to hers, and took his time kissing her once again. Her breath caught and she pressed even closer, kissing him back ardently. He swept his hands up and down her back, tracing the shape of her, bringing her ever nearer. Before this weekend, he had never imagined the two of them would be together like this. Now, convincing her to surrender long enough for him to stake his claim was all he could think about.

He didn't know what the future held. Didn't care. All

he was concerned about was Paige and the here and now. And right now, he wanted her. Needed her, needed this... more than he had ever needed anything in his life.

When Paige had decided to make love with Kurt, she'd told herself that she could separate her physical and emotional needs, could take what he offered without ever surrendering her whole self. Now, with their clothes coming off and his warm, strong hands exploring every inch of her skin, she wasn't so sure she'd be able to maintain her independence, at least not indefinitely. Especially when he worshiped her breasts, his lips and tongue suckling gently, until the tender friction was almost more than she could bear.

She'd sworn she would never give in to mere passion again.

Yet here she was, her back arching, her thighs parting, as fantasy became reality. And no wonder, she thought as her body heated and her emotions soared even higher. For the first time, she was making love with a man who was not only her former rival, but truly her equal, in so many ways....

And he, live-in-the-moment kind of guy that he was, seemed to be equally enthralled....

Murmuring his approval, Kurt sat on the edge of the bed and pulled her down to sit on his lap, so her knees were between his spread legs. She gasped, felt his arousal pressed against her hips. And then his hands were touching, exploring, stroking her intimately, until she was teetering on the edge of blissful oblivion.

Suddenly white-hot and needy, she vaulted off his lap and pulled him with her onto the bed. Laughing softly, he let her look her fill, even as he visually appreciated every inch of her. He was just as beautiful as she had always imagined. All satin skin and dark hair and hard male muscle. She could see how much he wanted her. And how much he cared about making this right, by the gentle determination and restraint in his gaze, in the way he made her feel so beautiful, so wanted and needed, in every way.

"We have as long as you need," he whispered.

As it turned out, she didn't need much.

Deliciously aroused, she trembled as he stretched out overtop of her, aware that nothing had ever felt so wonderful…or right. Wrapping her arms and legs around him, she lifted her hips to his. He penetrated her slowly, patiently, cupping her bottom with both hands, filling her with his heat and hardness. She made soft, breathless sounds of delight. He moaned, lifting her, going ever deeper. And then there was no stopping the pleasure. They were moving toward the same pinnacle, kissing and holding and taking each other with a hunger and a depth of emotion she hadn't known she possessed.

Blood rushed through her veins. Encompassed in hot, melting bliss, she plunged and bucked and rose with him, until finally it was too much for both of them. There was no holding back, no pretending this hadn't been meant to happen.…

Paige succumbed to his demands and relinquished control, joined him at the edge of ecstasy and beyond. And knew her life would never be the same again.

PAIGE LAY WITH HER ARMS wrapped around Kurt and her face buried in his solid shoulder, even after he shifted, moving onto his back, so her weight was draped over his. Their bodies were still humming with the pleasure they had just given one another. And she knew, despite all her earlier proclamations, that this was no simple fling. Not to her, anyway. She wanted Kurt the way she had never wanted any man, and wanting anyone like that scared the stuffing out of her. It left her feeling vulnerable. And for her, being vulnerable had always eventually led to being hurt....

"That was...amazing." Kurt's hoarse words were muffled against her hair.

Not trusting herself to speak just yet, without revealing even more, Paige nodded.

She had to find the strength to keep her guard up.

Before her heart went from just yearning for Kurt, to taking a fateful leap that would leave her completely exposed.

"Yes. But—" she forced herself to move away from the seductive cradle of his hard body "—we can't forget why we're here. Or how this is likely to end." She slipped from the bed, snatched up her clothes in one hand, and with an insouciance she couldn't begin to really feel, started to dress.

She had to protect herself.

Otherwise, she'd make the same mistake she had made before, and just turn to someone because she was in a stressful situation and feeling out of her element.

Yes, she and Kurt needed each other now. They were forced by circumstance to forget their differences and become a team. But that, too, would end. Sooner, maybe, than she wanted...

Kurt lay back, hands folded behind his head, his dark blue eyes watchful, and guarded now, too. "And how is this likely to end—in your view?" His words had a wary edge.

Paige drew a breath. Reassuring herself, despite her unprecedentedly passionate response to his lovemaking, that she was in no real danger of a broken heart—she was much too sophisticated and worldly wise for that—she countered equably, "With us going our separate ways."

His irises darkened. "How do you figure that?" he asked, calm and direct as ever.

"Well…" Paige squared her shoulders, drew a deep breath and said, with the least amount of jealousy she could, "The triplets' mother will be found eventually. And assuming you are the father, then you're going to have to make a decision." And it would be a tough one—she had no doubt.

Kurt's jaw set with McCabe resolve. He seemed to know where this conversation was going. "Camila and I are over," he stated flatly.

Paige zipped her jeans and sat down on the edge of the bed to put on her socks, then her boots. She paused to regard Kurt compassionately. "I know you think that now. But you haven't seen her in over a year and—"

He rose and, appearing irritated, began to dress, too. "That doesn't mean I'll fall in love with her when I do."

Paige watched him draw his jeans up his long, muscular legs. "It doesn't mean you won't, either."

He lifted a dissenting eyebrow. She ignored the warning glare and plunged on, drawing on her expertise as a physician to counsel knowledgably. "Something happens to parents when they share the birth of a child, even those who previously weren't getting along. They're bonded in an almost magical way that, as a pediatric specialist, I have seen over and over again."

Kurt pulled on his shirt. Leaving the edges open, to reveal a chest that was every bit as masculine and appealing as the rest of him, he sauntered closer, put his hands on her shoulders. "Just like you and I are bonded right now."

Paige swallowed and tipped her head back, to better look into his eyes. "Yes," she replied implacably. "Only I'm not the triplets' mother, and you may be their father." Her heart ached at the knowledge. "And when we take me out of this situation and bring another woman into the mix, you could very well want to be with her."

Kurt clasped her shoulders more tightly, and his expression went from brooding to inscrutable in a flash. "Or not."

A thrill swept through Paige as she recalled how passionately and tenderly he had just made love to her. She had a growing sensation that, if the decision were left to him, he'd soon be doing it again. An action, she told herself sternly, that would only complicate matters further.

Out of self-preservation, she slipped from his hold and stepped away. "And let's not forget the practical aspects of the situation." She found her brush and ran it through the tousled waves of her hair. "You and I have both learned firsthand how difficult it is to take care of all three children at once." She exhaled. "I don't know how mothers do it if they have to manage triplets completely on their own." She paused. "Maybe that's why the girls' mom gave them up. And if that's the case, it also means that she could change her mind if the situation improves, and she suddenly finds herself able to get the help she's needed all along. From you, your family, the entire McCabe clan."

Kurt couldn't argue about that.

Met by his grim silence, Paige swallowed. "Would you be okay with splitting responsibility for the kids with their mom?" She paused to study his demeanor once again. "Or would you feel you had to get married to the babies' mom, do the honorable thing?"

PRIOR TO THIS, Kurt would have automatically said yes, he would get married to any woman who found herself pregnant with his child. Now, suspecting Camila was the mom, knowing how he felt about the kids—and how he was beginning to feel about Paige—he wasn't sure a forced marriage was the right thing to do. He also knew Paige deserved a brutally honest response, even if it wasn't what she wanted to hear.

He edged closer, buttoning his shirt. "Theoretically— if I thought I could get along with the triplets' mom, and I had no one else in my life—then sure, I would automatically do the right thing and propose. But if it was going to be a bitter environment—" *the way it had been when he and Camila split* "—I think it would be better to arrange for the children to have my name, legally, and work out something else. Like divorced parents do. Without the marriage."

Kurt watched Paige slowly put down her hairbrush.

"And that bothers you?"

She picked up a stick of lip gloss and applied it to her soft, kiss-swollen lips, then said, just as carefully, "I'm glad you wouldn't marry someone simply for the sake of propriety—'cause I don't think that kind of thing ever works. At least, not from what I've seen."

Worry still clouded her eyes.

"But…?" Kurt pressed.

She lifted her slender shoulders in a delicate shrug. "Even if you're not still in love, having a baby with someone is a really romantic thing."

Kurt was as pleased by Paige's obvious jealousy and possessiveness as he was disheartened by her lack of faith in him. "Let's say we *do* prove Camila's the mom. You're worried that romance will lead me back to her," he guessed.

"It could be why she left the babies here, because she wanted you to get to know the triplets and then do the honorable thing by recommitting to her."

"Or maybe she was tired of the responsibility, and simply wanted to hand it off to me and my family permanently. We won't know until we track her down. And thus far—" Kurt pressed his palm to his chest "—all *my* efforts have failed."

Compassion crept into Paige's low tone. "You tried again today?"

"Several times, on email and by phone," Kurt admitted with mounting frustration, glad they were on the same page about this much. "I got nowhere."

Paige looked down at his hand, but didn't twine her fingers with his. "Do you want me to ask my parents if they can find her?"

He nodded in relief. The sooner they cleared this up, the sooner he would be able to sort things out with Paige.

Figure out where they went from here. "If you could," he said firmly, "that would be great."

"OF COURSE WE'D BE HAPPY to help locate Camila Albright," Paige's mom said, after Paige had called to fill her in. "What I don't understand is why you're making such an effort to help Kurt McCabe track down his ex-girlfriend. I thought the two of you couldn't stand each other."

"Yes, well..." Paige grimaced, as she met Kurt's eyes. "It, um, turns out he's not as bad as I originally thought."

Kurt's chest shook with silent chuckles.

"Really!" Dani said cheerfully.

Paige swung away from Kurt's mirthful expression. "Don't make more of it than there is," she warned her mother hastily, glad she wasn't there to see her flush. It was bad enough that Kurt was. Paige raked her fingers through her hair, shifting it away from her face. "I'm just doing him a favor. So he'll owe me," she added, with a touch of her previous rancor for the handsome veterinarian.

Kurt made another face—this one designed to make her laugh.

"Ah, that sounds more like it," her mom teased. "So what are you up to this weekend?"

Obviously, Paige thought in relief, her parents hadn't heard about her foster-mother gig. Which was no surprise. With her dad involved in the editing of a film, her mom trying to finish a book, her parents were a little out of the loop with local goings-on.

"Uh, just...you know...the usual weekend stuff,"

Paige fibbed. And some not so usual stuff. Like taking care of three babies—and making love to the impossibly sexy Kurt McCabe.

There was a short silence, during which Paige could almost feel her mother's suspicion that something was a little off, though she couldn't put her finger on precisely what. Only that Paige was calling her at ten-thirty on a Saturday night, to ask a favor....

"Anyway, Mom—" Paige drew a deep, enervating breath "—if you and or Dad could use your connections and look into this..."

"Will do," Dani promised. "Although I have to warn you, it will likely take at least a day or so to find out what you and Kurt want to know."

"No problem," she said. For reasons she preferred not to admit, she really wasn't in a hurry to find Camila. At least not until Monday morning...when life was supposed to return to normal.

"And Mom?" Paige said, finally collecting herself. "Thanks for helping." She hung up. Turned to see Kurt studying her, less happily now.

"Your parents don't know you're here, do they?"

"Obviously not," Paige answered drily.

Kurt rubbed a thumb across the sensitive skin inside her wrist. "Why didn't you tell them?"

She felt the tingles all the way down to her knees. Trembling, she tried to move back. "No reason."

He held on, when she would have danced away. "There's a reason."

Paige narrowed her eyes. "I thought you were going to try and mind your own business."

He looked at her quizzically. "Did I say that?"

Now that she thought about it…not exactly. Paige shrugged and tried not to tremble at the gentle intimacy of his touch. "You should have."

His gaze radiated all the tenderness of his earlier lovemaking. Still holding her wrist, and wrapping his other arm about her waist, he brought her flush against him. "Hasn't anyone told you?" he murmured. "You are my business."

Excitement sifted through her. "Kurt…"

He lowered his head and kissed her slowly, deliberately. Until her toes curled in her boots and every rational thought left her head.

Her body had the consistency of melted butter when he finally stopped and rubbed the dampness from her lower lip with the pad of his thumb. "So how come you don't want them to know you're here with me and my kids?"

The intensity of his gaze held her in place as surely as the tenderness of his touch and the heat of his kiss. Even more boundaries dissolved. She found herself answering honestly, "Because they'd probably worry unnecessarily." And one thing never changed, no matter how old she got. Paige hated to worry her folks.

Kurt blinked and let go of her. "Why?"

She used the opportunity to put distance between them. "I'm an only child. They're protective in the extreme."

Kurt walked over to build up the fire in the grate. "Why would they think you need sheltering?"

Watching, Paige edged closer to the flames. "My mom would conclude I'd get attached to the babies and get my heart broken when I had to give them up." A prediction that was so close to the truth it wasn't funny.

Kurt put the poker back in the stand and replaced the fireplace screen. "And your dad?"

Wishing his tall, muscular frame didn't make her feel so feminine in his presence, Paige answered his query with a wry twist to her lips. "My dad would definitely question your motives if he knew you'd made love to me." *And probably want to take you off for some old-fashioned man-to-man talk about your "intentions."* Paige didn't even want to think how that would go.

Her mom and dad might have had an unusual start to their own courtship, when they were in their thirties— with a marriage in Mexico that neither could initially recall—but her folks were all about tradition and commitment now. They wanted to see her settled down and married.

Kurt studied Paige with a brooding look. "What about you? Do you question my motives?"

She flushed under his scrutiny. "No. I know why you did what you did."

His lips thinned. "And why is that?"

Was it her imagination or was there a raw edge of hope in his expression? "For the same reason we discussed earlier." Paige held his level gaze with effort. "Because situations like this have you reaching out to whomever is closest. And right now," she admitted sadly, "that person is me."

Chapter Seven

Kurt wished he could dispute what Paige had claimed, but the truth was, they were in this together. Caring for the triplets had bonded them in an unexpected way. It had shown him a side of Paige he had never suspected existed. He imagined she felt the same about him.

He also sensed there was more than that drawing them to one another. Much more. The problem was, how could he convince Paige of that? Or make her want more than a one-time fling, as he did?

He had no answer to his dilemma as they bathed the triplets, with slightly better results this time. Or when they fed them another bottle, played with them and finally got them to sleep again. Or when he and Paige fell, exhausted, into separate beds around 2:00 a.m.

When they all woke at six, the girls were so ravenous it took everything he and Paige had to get their bottles heated, all three diapers changed and the girls fed before there was a mass revolt.

"I think we're beginning to get the hang of this," Paige murmured at long last. Seated cross-legged on the floor, next to a quilt they'd spread out, she faced

Lindsay, Lori and Lucille. All three were waving their arms and smiling.

Happy for the camaraderie, Kurt settled next to Paige, facing the babies. "The girls seem to think so, too."

Paige turned to him. "Can you tell them apart— without looking at their bracelets?"

Able to envision many more mornings just like this, Kurt shrugged. "I've been trying."

"So have I," Paige lamented, with a teasing half smile. "With mixed results."

He studied her feminine profile. "Do you think that's why the bracelets were put on? Because their mother can't tell them apart, either?"

"Maybe." Paige leaned forward to hand Lucille a rattle. "It could just as easily be a fashion statement, though." She tucked an infant-size soft cotton bunny in Lori's palm. "I see a lot of infants with pierced ears."

Kurt gave Lindsay a squeaking cloth snail. "So do I," he said. "But gold ID bracelets? I haven't seen anyone wear one of those since college."

Paige's eyes widened. "They wore them at A&M?"

Kurt noted how thick and long her auburn lashes were. "The girls in one of the sororities all did."

Lazily, Paige stretched her calves and wiggled her toes. "What about Camila? Did she wear one?"

He shook his head. "She liked ankle bracelets. A navel ring and earrings. I never saw her wear anything on her wrist."

Kurt tore his eyes from the graceful slope of Paige's neck, the delicate shell of her ear. "You couldn't really put an ankle bracelet on a baby and expect it to be seen."

He stretched his pajama-clad legs out next to hers. "Their booties or sleepers would get in the way."

"True." Paige turned her attention back to the three infants and grinned. "Lindsay seems to smile more readily than the other two. And Lori is the most impatient."

Kurt flashed her a crooked smile. "And Lucille seems to be the most physically agile."

Paige bit her lower lip. "But they all look alike." Her brow furrowed as they continued to study the babies. "Did your parents ever have trouble telling you and Kyle, or your three brothers, apart?"

Kurt turned his attention back to her. "My mom said they did when we were babies. As we grew up, our differing personalities made it easy to differentiate between us."

Gentle light came into Paige's eyes. "I can understand that. I always felt the same way about you and Kyle."

Kurt warmed to the affection in her voice. "So what does my behavior tell you?" He caught her hand in his.

She glanced down at their entwined fingers, but made no effort to pull away. "You're very kind and loving with animals and kids."

"And the rest of the time?" he prodded.

"For me?" Paige wrinkled her nose mischievously. "Trouble with a capital T!" She withdrew her hand, sat back. "How would you describe my personality?"

It was his chance to show her he did understand her. Kurt searched for one word that most adequately captured his sense of her. Finally, he said, "I'd say you were serious—because you try to do everything perfectly every time."

Paige sighed. "True."

But that wasn't all, Kurt thought. "And you're sophisticated," he said, gratified to see her defenses melt a little more. "Part of that is because of who your parents are—the fact you've gone back and forth between Hollywood and Laramie and wherever else in the world your dad happened to be directing or starring in a movie since you were a kid. And the other part of it is because you are by nature a very elegant, very graceful lady."

Her soft, appreciative laughter filled the room. "Why, Kurt." Paige batted her eyelashes and did her best Scarlet O'Hara imitation. "I do declare, you're almost complimentary this morning."

With good reason. He wanted her to know how attracted he was to her. He wanted her to see him as something other than the irritating rival from her youth. He held up a warning finger. "And don't even get me started on those flannel pajamas."

"Okay." Paige rolled her eyes and shook her head. "Here come the insults I know and love."

He caught her hand and kissed the back of it. "I'm serious. I love the way you look in them." All soft and womanly.

Paige squared her slim shoulders. "I can't believe you're hitting on me when we haven't even had a cup of coffee yet."

If he'd had his way, and they'd been alone, they would still be in bed. Together. Making love again, slowly and ardently. But sensing he had already moved too far, too fast, Kurt forced himself to back up to the flirtation stage of the relationship. "Speaking of which, how about I rustle us up some breakfast?"

She tilted her head, mocking him with a look. "You can cook?"

Remembering when he had said pretty much the same thing to her, Kurt winked. "I have a few tricks up my sleeve."

HALF AN HOUR LATER, Paige pushed her empty plate away. "That was delicious." *Unlike what she had cooked for him,* she couldn't help but think wryly. She met his eyes admiringly. "It takes real skill to make perfect sunny-side-up eggs, bacon and toast."

Kurt looked down at her in mock seriousness. "Either that or it's just the process of doing it a few thousand times. Not only is bacon and eggs good at any time of the day or night, it's one of the few meals I know how to rustle up that doesn't involve removing a plastic wrapper and sticking it in the microwave."

"I hate to say it but you're being way too modest." The bacon had been crisp, the toast golden-brown and crunchy. Even the yolks had been done perfectly. Not too runny, not too hard. "You could put a five-star-restaurant chef to shame with that meal."

He grinned as happily as if she had invited him into her bedroom. "Want another cup of coffee?"

"Yes, thank you."

Glancing up at him, Paige couldn't help but note that he looked impossibly sexy in white-and-gray-striped cotton pajama pants, a navy T-shirt and shearling-lined moccasins. His dark hair had that rumpled just-out-of-bed look. His handsome face was lined with a stubble that came from twenty-four hours without a razor. His only commitment to grooming so far that morning had been to brush his teeth and swig peppermint mouthwash. She knew because she had rushed to do the same the first chance she'd got.

Kurt sauntered back to her side, topped off her cup with tranquil efficiency. "So what do you want to do next?" he asked lazily.

Keep flirting. See where it leads... Ignoring the tidal wave of heat starting deep inside her, she reined herself in. Forced herself to use every ounce of her common sense and play it safe this time.

Taking a quick, bolstering sip of coffee, she stood. "Probably laundry. I noticed this morning we were down to the last two sets of clean clothes for the girls."

Fortunately, Paige soon discovered, Annie McCabe had an extralarge washer, and everything the girls had was pastel, so they were able to put it all in one load. Because Kurt's mother had other grandchildren, she even had baby detergent on hand.

Finished, they had just started back for the kitchen when the doorbell rang. And rang again. A cacophony of excited voices sounded on the front porch, and the triplets began to stir in their buggy from all the commotion. Kurt groaned. With one glance out the window, Paige knew why.

"Looking good, little brother," Trevor McCabe remarked, striding in after Kurt opened the door wide.

"Yeah, Kyle said you hadn't had any sleep, but obviously that's changed," Tyler McCabe added.

Teddy McCabe slapped Kurt on the back as he passed. "Triplets, huh? That's the first for our generation."

"Hey, Paige," the McCabe triplets said in unison.

Before she knew it, she was engulfed in hugs from Kurt's three older brothers, their wives and then their kids. As if not wanting to be left out, Lindsay, Lori and Lucille let out a collective wail.

Lots of oohing and ahhing followed.

The girls were quickly picked up and soothed with the tranquility of experienced parents. Kurt went to make more coffee. Additional food was brought in by the McCabe women. Casseroles, salads, fresh fruit, milk, more coffee and every perishable item they could have asked for.

Rebecca—Trevor's wife—said, "It's really great what you're doing here. Letting Kurt be near his kids."

Susie—Tyler's wife—added more cautiously, "Not that we know for sure. Yet."

"Yeah," Amy—Teddy's wife—declared with customary optimism, "but why else would anyone leave the triplets with Kurt? Unless they were McCabes?"

There was a murmur of assent as all three women worked together to put the food away. "Looks like you've already had breakfast," Rebecca said, "but this breakfast casserole will be good tomorrow, too."

"Have you all eaten?" Paige asked. As long as they were here, she didn't mind feeding everyone. Even if she was still in her pajamas!

"Hours ago." Amy waved off the offer. "We McCabes are up at dawn."

Trevor strode in and headed straight for the coffee, stopping to give his wife a hug as he went. "You shouldn't be waiting on Kurt and fixing him breakfast," he told Paige.

"Actually, he fixed it," she replied.

"Paige made dinner for us last night," Kurt interjected, strolling in with Lucille in his arms. Teddy carried Lori, and Tyler held Lindsay.

"And it was an unqualified disaster," Paige admitted with a self-conscious blush, figuring if the news was going to come out, she was going to be the one to tell it. The only way she knew to save face was to make light of what, for her, still served as a major source of embarrassment.

"I find that hard to believe," Teddy said gently.

Believe it, Paige thought. "I breaded the beef in confectioner's sugar."

Laughter erupted, the sound so good-hearted and empathetic that Paige put aside her usual need to be perfect and continued making fun of herself. "It was really awful!"

More good-natured laughter followed.

"Paige is exaggerating." To her surprise, Kurt leaped to her defense. He flashed her a sexy grin. "It was actually very good—kind of Asian-Southern fusion."

She rolled her eyes at him. "That's very kind of you to say, but it's not at all true!" And he did not need to protect her from this humiliation. "Even the cream gravy was sweet! It might as well have been frosting."

More laughter followed, along with tales of other culinary mishaps from everyone there. Half an hour later, they were still holding their stomachs and wiping tears of hilarity from their eyes. Paige had never felt so blessed, or included. Whoever had left the triplets with the McCabe clan had known what they were doing, she realized. Everyone should have this. And the Thanksgiving holiday coming up in a few days made the situation even more poignant.

Rebecca and Trevor's seven-year-old twins came into the kitchen. Jenny and Joshua went straight for Kurt, one hanging on each side of him. "Are the babies going to be at Thanksgiving dinner, Uncle Kurt?" Joshua asked.

He smiled. "Um...I'm not sure yet. I hope so."

"Us, too." Jenny stood on one foot, then the other. "Can they eat pumpkin pie?"

"Not yet."

The twins turned to Paige. "Our mommy said you are those babies' foster mommy."

"For the moment, yes, I am," Paige agreed. And it hurt her to realize that was almost over, too.

Joshua's red eyebrows arched. "Are you and Uncle Kurt married?"

"Um, no," Kurt answered.

The freckles stood out on Jenny's face as she looked from him to Paige. "Then how come you have babies?"

"Right now, we're just taking care of them," Paige said.

Both twins looked at her uncomprehendingly.

"They are not actually my children," she continued.

Joshua scratched his head. "Are they Uncle Kurt's then?"

Kurt smiled. "We're still trying to figure that out. It's complicated."

"So complicated I don't think we should have any more questions. In fact, I think we all ought to be going," Rebecca said firmly, marshaling her kids toward the door.

Susie nodded and signaled to her two children, as well. She looked at Paige and Kurt. "You'll tell us if you need anything?"

"We will," he said. "Thank you."

More activity followed as the triplets were settled back in their buggy once again, and jackets were found. Goodbyes said, Kurt walked his siblings and their families out, while Paige wheeled the babies gently back and forth. By the time Kurt came back inside and shed the jacket he'd thrown on over his pajamas, the triplets were fast asleep.

"Good work," he said with a smile, taking a long, tender look at the kids. He turned back to her.

And finally, she had to ask. "What are we doing?"

PAIGE HADN'T MEANT TO blurt that out. Now that she had, however, it was too late to take it back. "We're behaving like the triplets are ours."

Kurt leaned close enough to kiss her—but didn't. "They will be soon."

"We don't even know for sure that they are *yours*."

His eyes roamed her face with disturbing intensity, lingering on her lips for a heart-stopping moment before returning to her eyes. "I have to believe they were left with me for a reason."

Paige studied him, wanting to understand Kurt completely. "Because they needed a daddy."

"Because they were meant to bring me to you."

Silence fell. He took her in his arms. "I care about those little girls, Paige. And I also care about you." He tightened his hold on her possessively. "And unless I'm wrong, you feel the same way."

She swallowed. "Of course those three babies have stolen my heart. They're so adorable. Who wouldn't fall in love with them? But as for you and me…" She splayed her hands across the solid warmth of his chest. "I still think we're getting way ahead of ourselves here."

The look he gave her was direct. "I'm willing to slow down."

Paige shook her head imperiously. "How about call a halt?"

He merely smiled at her and continued looking at her in a way that made her feel all hot and bothered inside. "I'm not going to pretend I don't want you."

"Then how about not showing it quite as much then?" she said, knowing the less time they spent together in an intimate fashion, the better. Their situation was complicated enough without bringing sex back into the equation.

He tucked a strand of hair behind her ear and studied her quietly. "Would that make you feel better?"

Paige drew in a short, stabilizing breath, deciding in this case it would be best to be blunt. "I'm a cautious person, Kurt, when it comes to getting emotionally involved with anyone or anything."

His blue eyes glimmered mischievously. "And I'm an 'if it feels right do it' type."

Steeling herself against any advances he might make, she regarded him in silence, knowing for both their sakes this was one battle she simply had to win.

He grinned and released her. "But for you I will try to curb those impulses."

Trying not to feel too bereft at the sudden absence of his touch, Paige nodded deferentially. "Thank you," she said with all the politeness she could muster. She worked to slow her racing pulse. "Now if you don't mind—" she looked him in the eye "—I'd like to take a shower and get dressed while I still have a chance."

AN HOUR LATER, Paige was taking the baby clothes out of the dryer when the doorbell rang again. Kurt went off to get it. Seconds later, she winced as she heard two voices she would have preferred not to hear coming through the ranch house. With an overflowing basket of baby clothes in her hands, Paige met her mother and father in the living room. As always, they made a handsome couple, her beautiful mother every bit as attractive as her movie-star dad.

"Why didn't you tell us?" Dani demanded, running a hand through her upswept, strawberry-blond hair.

Because I had a feeling you would overreact, Paige thought, lowering the basket to the sofa. "How did you hear?"

Beau gave Paige and Kurt a long measuring look—and as always, saw too much. "Your mother and I went into town to run some errands this afternoon." He frowned in reproach. "You can imagine our surprise when we found out nearly everyone knew about the triplets that were left on your doorstep."

"Except us," Dani said quietly, disappointment radiating in her gaze.

Guilt flooded Paige. She hadn't meant to hurt her parents' feelings. She had been trying to protect them. "Sorry about that," she murmured. "It's been a little hectic."

Dani walked over to peek inside the buggy. The

triplets were still snuggled together, sleeping soundly. "I imagine so." Her expression rife with tenderness, she turned back to Paige. "It still doesn't explain why you failed to tell us you were becoming a foster mother."

"It was an emergency situation. And it's just temporary. As soon as we confirm who the babies' mother is, we'll be able to get them into a more permanent situation. Which brings me to my next question." Ignoring their unconvinced looks, Paige hurried on. "Have you been able to use your connections to find out where Camila Albright is?"

Beau nodded. "I talked to her agent. Apparently, she's been in seclusion most of the last year, working on a screenplay. She's now at the Four Seasons hotel in Dallas, room 612, working on preproduction rewrites. I left word with her agent that Kurt has been trying to get in touch with her. Her agent said he would pass the message along to Camila, via voice mail and email, but he wasn't optimistic she would call him back. As usual, when she's knee-deep in a project, she's not accepting any calls."

"Thank you for locating her," Kurt said sincerely.

"Is Camila the mother of these babies?" Beau asked him, point-blank.

Kurt spread his hands wide. "If they are my children, as the note that was left with them seems to indicate, then Camila has to be their mother."

"And if not?" Dani pressed.

"Then I have no idea who they belong to," he admitted with a grimace.

"Which is why we have law enforcement and social services involved in the search," Paige explained.

"Well, I hope you get this cleared up soon. In the meantime, what are you going to do about your work at the hospital?" Beau asked his daughter.

"We're meeting with the social worker and Kurt's brother Kyle again tomorrow to see where the investigation is, and to decide what to do next. Hopefully, we'll have answers by then. In the meantime, I've already asked for Monday off," Paige said.

"Same here," Kurt added.

"Well…" Dani breathed a sigh of relief. "We're glad you are helping out. Obviously, it's the charitable thing to do."

"But?" Paige prodded, guessing there was more.

"The situation you are in right now…living together, taking care of these three tiny orphans…is more fantasy than reality."

"It's sort of like playing house, grown-up style," Beau said, direct and to the point as ever, when it came to protecting his only child's interests.

Dani shot her husband a look that said *tread lightly here*. Then turned back to Paige. "We're concerned, because we can see how you could easily fall in love with these babies and want to do more than just be their temporary mom."

Wasn't that the understatement of the year, Paige thought wearily. She held up a hand. "I'm not going to get my heart broken here, Mom. So you don't have to worry about that, either, Dad."

"Good." Beau's expression was grim. "Because as heart wrenching as this situation no doubt is, it's not what you've wanted for yourself," he reminded her sternly. "And we don't want you to get so caught up in what is essentially Kurt and Child Protective Service's problem that you forget the dream you have been holding on to all these years."

Paige got their message. "Or in other words, don't settle—" *for less than absolute perfection* "—when I could still marry my very own Mr. Right and have it all."

Her parents nodded in unison. "In the meantime, let us know what is happening or if there's anything else we can do, Paige."

She nodded in turn, wishing she didn't have so much to live up to. "I will."

Beau looked at Kurt. "You make sure Paige doesn't get hurt by all of this."

To her relief, he accepted her dad's warning with the seriousness with which it was given. "Yes, sir," he said.

Kurt and Paige walked them out, said goodbye. As they came back inside, he turned to her. "Your parents don't have a clue about your plans to have a family the new-fashioned way. Do they?"

Chapter Eight

Paige's need to conceal her every vulnerability resurfaced. "You can't say that surprises you."

"I guess not, given that you haven't confided anything else to them about that part of your life." Kurt held her gaze. "I just thought you were a lot closer to them."

Unwilling to contemplate what it would be like if he decided he wanted to understand every aspect of her life, Paige drew an unsteady breath. She wasn't used to that level of intimacy with the men she dated, and she wasn't sure she wanted to experience it. Hating the defensive way his questions made her feel, she clamped her arms in front of her like a shield. "I am close to them, in a lot of ways. I can talk to them about my work, and my career aspirations and their work…and I enjoy spending time with them."

Kurt propped his hands on his hips and frowned. "But?" he prodded, his dark brows drawing together when she failed to go on.

Paige checked on the babies, found them still fast asleep. Needing something to concentrate on other than Kurt's sexy male presence, she gathered up the bottles and took them into the kitchen. "Maybe it's the pressure of being an only child, and the apple of their eyes. But my parents think I'm perfect, and I've never liked disappointing them. Plus, as you know," she continued, "they are both career superstars, in their own right."

Kurt searched her face. "So you feel you *have* to be perfect," he murmured.

Paige was glad he understood the pressure she felt. That made it easier for her to continue confiding in him. She flashed a rueful smile. "It's a self-imposed standard, not anything that comes from my parents. But…" She couldn't seem to let go of her need to please them. Aware Kurt was still watching her, she shrugged and finished, "What can you do?"

He continued to regard her thoughtfully, clearly intrigued. "Let them know you're human? That like everyone else, you don't always get exactly what you want?" He lounged against the counter, facing her. "And in those cases, have to make do?"

He made it sound so easy. Paige sent him a sidelong glance as she emptied the bottles and rinsed them, before filling the sink with hot soapy water. The she sighed, wishing she didn't desperately want to kiss him again. "Is that how it is in your family?" she asked, curious to know the more intimate details of his own life.

Kurt plucked a clean dish towel out of the drawer, then watched as she picked up a bottle brush, then scrubbed and rinsed each bottle. "My mom had triplets—all boys." He took the bottle Paige handed to him, and wiped it dry. The wintry fragrance of his cologne stirred her senses.

Kurt continued solemnly, "Mom's first husband decided it was too much to handle, and walked out on her. Shortly after their divorce, her dad died and she had to take over the struggling family ranch, while she was simultaneously trying to start her own business and bring Teddy, Trevor and Tyler up on her own."

"That sounds incredibly hard," Paige murmured.

Kurt nodded. "According to my mom, it was. Luckily, my dad came into the picture to help with the ranch—and eventually the triplets—and he and Mom fell in love. After they married, they had me and Kyle."

Kurt's fingers brushed hers as he accepted another wet, clean bottle. He paused and grinned. "So it's safe to say our childhoods were pretty lively—in a good way."

Aware how comforting it was to hang out with him, and wishing they had done so years ago, Paige smiled. "After a few days with the triplets," she murmured, "I can only imagine what your household must have been like." There definitely would have been a lot of chaos, but also a lot of fun, a lot of love.…

Kurt sobered as he walked over to get a gallon jug of bottled water and the powdered infant formula mix. "Anyway, my point is it's always great when you really excel at something. But there was also a lot of latitude for failure in our family. Because some of the most valuable lessons are learned when you don't initially meet a goal, and have to pick yourself up, dust yourself off and try all over again."

Together, they mixed half a dozen bottles of formula and slid them into the fridge.

"It sounds a lot more laid-back than my childhood." Paige returned to let the water out of the sink.

Taking her hand and locking his eyes with hers, Kurt

reflected quietly, "It was and it wasn't. There's not a lot of downtime on a cattle ranch, and back then, my brothers and I worked alongside Dad and all the hired hands."

He drew her closer, until they were standing near enough to feel one another's body heat.

"And when we weren't doing that, we were busy helping Mom out with her business," he continued. "Going with her to trade shows and working at the new product testing center."

Just as Paige had often gone with her dad on location, or accompanied her mother on business to Los Angeles and New York.

But they digressed by focusing on the past…instead of concentrating on the future.

Paige ignored the intensity in Kurt's gaze and the soft, compelling sound of his voice, and forced herself to be practical. "Speaking of trying again… Now that we know where Camila is, what's going to be your next move?"

He didn't have to think twice. "I want to drive to Dallas with you and the kids. Check into the Four Seasons Hotel—where she's staying—and see her."

Paige's heartbeat picked up a notch. It reassured her to be included, and it also scared her. This was beginning to feel as much her problem as it was his, and common sense told her that her parents were correct on this one point. What happened to the triplets—whether they stayed with Kurt, went back to their birth mother or managed to end up with both—was not her dilemma.

Nevertheless, the sooner a solution was found, the sooner she would be free to pursue her own dreams of having a child of her own. Paige peered up at him, studying the lines of his handsome face. "Are you sure you don't want to go on your own?"

Kurt shook his head. "I need to see Camila's reaction when she sees the kids—and they see her—to get a true idea of where things stand."

That made sense. Still… "That's a long drive."

"Nearly three hours," Kurt affirmed, with the steadfast determination she was beginning to know so well. He glanced at his watch. "If we leave now, we could be there by around 8:00 or 9:00 p.m."

Thanks to Kurt's brother Kyle, they already had car seats installed in her station wagon. All they'd really have to do was pack up and go. Which led them to the next set of problems to be solved. "What if Camila isn't at the hotel when we arrive?"

Kurt shrugged, unconcerned. "Then we'll wait until she is. But since she likes to work in the evenings, and she's apparently in the midst of a work deadline, it's likely she will be there."

LUCKILY FOR THEM, the buggy folded flat and was able to be fit in the cargo area of Paige's station wagon. The triplets' suitcase full of belongings and extra diapers sat on top of that. Because space was limited, Kurt and Paige opted to share a small overnight bag.

It felt oddly intimate, putting her pajamas, toiletries and a fresh change of clothes on top of his.

Paige shook off the emotion. This was just a temporary situation. Nothing more.

If they were lucky, it would be over sooner than she thought.

Unfortunately, the trip was not as easy as they had hoped. The triplets woke halfway there, hungry and wet, and Paige and Kurt had to pull over in a gas station parking lot, and manage the bottles and diaper changes in the car. The whole process took more than an hour, but once they were on the road again, the motion of the vehicle put the girls back to sleep. And they were still dozing as Kurt and Paige checked in to their quarters on the third floor of the hotel. The suite had a living room with a sofa bed and chairs, an adjacent bedroom with a king-size bed, and a luxurious marble bathroom.

"So how do you want to do this?" Paige asked, after the bellboy left.

"How about we just take the buggy up to her room right now?"

Paige knew it was an intrusion. She also felt a lot would be learned from looking at Camila when she and the babies came face-to-face. So she agreed.

Together, she and Kurt headed for the elevators. Five minutes later, they were standing with the buggy in front of Camila's room. Kurt knocked on the door to 612. Once, twice. Finally, it opened.

Camila stood there in stylish designer sweats. Her long black hair was pulled into a ponytail. A pair of trendy red reading glasses framed her bright blue eyes. Her voluptuous lips opened into an O of surprise, but amazement turned quickly to annoyance. Her thin black brows lowered as she looked from Kurt to Paige to the baby buggy turned so she could see inside.

Camila sighed. Shook her head as if that would clear it. After gazing down at the babies for a brief moment, she peered up and down the hall, as if searching for hidden cameras. "Am I being punked? Because if I am, I have to tell you, Kurt McCabe, this is really lousy timing. And—" Camila turned to Paige "—I would have thought you, being the daughter of Dani and Beau Chamberlain, would have better sense than to get involved in whatever this is."

She certainly seemed innocent, Paige thought.

Kurt stared at Camila, still judging, assessing. "You're really going to tell me you know nothing about these triplets?" he demanded in a low, stern tone.

She lifted her shoulders in a shrug. "Should I?" she asked in obvious confusion.

Wanting to speed up the denouement, Paige took a more blunt approach. "I think what Kurt is trying to ask is, are the babies yours?"

Camila snorted. "Absolutely not!"

"You're sure?" Kurt pressed.

"I think I'd know if I'd given birth to triplets," she replied sarcastically, then paused at the bewildered expression on his face. Her defensive posture eased, and a mixture of compassion and curiosity replaced her annoyance. "Is this why you've been pestering me nonstop all weekend?"

Paige and Kurt nodded.

"What's going on?" Camila asked with something akin to sympathy.

Looking relieved that she had let her guard down enough to talk with him, Kurt explained the events thus far.

Camila listened quietly, her expression serious and thoughtful. Finally, she said, "It wasn't me. But for the record, Kurt? Just so you know… If I had been pregnant, I certainly would have told you."

"WELL, NOW WE KNOW," Kurt murmured finally when they got back to the room.

The girls stirred slightly. Paige pushed the buggy back and forth until they lapsed into slumber once again, then walked over to the hotel window where Kurt stood. His hands shoved in the pockets of his jeans, his lips set disconsolately, he looked out at the gray November skies above the beautifully manicured golf course.

"So if they aren't Camila's…" Paige had believed Kurt's ex when she'd said they weren't.

"Then Lindsay, Lori and Lucille aren't my daughters. They can't be," Kurt finished grimly.

An even deeper silence fell. Paige understood his dejection, after all they had been through. She felt it, too. "Is it possible someone mixed you up with Kyle?" she prodded, still hoping there was a way to make this situation turn out the way the triplets' mommy had wanted. "The two of you are identical twins…and he's a member of law enforcement. So maybe the mother wanted to leave the children to be raised by him."

Certainly Kyle had a heroic streak, too. And a reputation for having a heart as big as all Texas.

"I don't know. Maybe." Kurt exhaled and reached for his cell phone. He punched in a number, then waited. When Kyle answered, Kurt put the call on speakerphone so Paige could listen, and brought his brother up to speed. "*Is* there any chance they're yours?" Kurt asked.

"To tell you the truth, the kids are so cute, I kind of

wish I could claim them as mine," Kyle admitted gruffly. "But there's no chance of it being so. I wasn't seeing anyone in that time period."

So where, Paige wondered, did they go from here?

"How is the investigation going on your end?" Kurt asked.

"There's still no report of missing or kidnapped children, but I'm calling the state Bureau of Vital Statistics as soon as they open tomorrow morning. If the triplets were born in Texas and their birth was legally recorded, we should know the identity of one or both parents tomorrow morning. And be able to go from there."

"CAN'T SLEEP?"

The soft voice brought him out of his reverie.

Kurt turned to see Paige coming toward him. In a pair of pink-and-white-striped flannel pajamas and bare feet, her hair tousled, she looked sexier than ever, as well as concerned. Trying not to think how much he welcomed her gentle compassion, or how quickly the situation was bringing them together, he countered, just as quietly, "I thought you were asleep."

She locked gazes and moved toward him. "Too much on my mind."

And mine, Kurt thought, inhaling her lavender perfume.

Paige came closer. "You haven't said much about what happened earlier with Camila."

What was there to say? Trying not to fantasize about what it would be like to be with Paige all the time, Kurt moved away from the window and turned on a lamp. The additional illumination made him all the more conscious of her.

He turned his glance away from the soft swell of her breasts and the hint of cleavage visible beneath the V-neck. Tense with worry and edgy with sexual frustration, he shrugged. "It's obvious the triplets aren't my kids."

Her green eyes softened in understanding. "But you want them to be."

Just as I'd like us to be together without problems or complication...or anything but the pleasure of the here and now, Kurt thought. But that wasn't going to happen. Paige was the kind of woman who needed a precision in her life that came from never deviating from her vision of how things should be. That wasn't him—never had been, never would be. And in the meantime, he had to figure out how to deal with the truth of what they'd learned about the triplets' parentage.

He worked to keep the disappointment from his voice, giving her his sometimes-life-sucks-and-you-just-have-to-deal-with-it scowl. "You'd like the girls to be yours, too," he told her in mounting aggravation. "It doesn't make it so."

Paige raised her chin. "Whoever left the kids at the ranch wanted you to have them."

Kurt tensed. "But did that person have the right to do so?"

She stared at him, clearly not comprehending where he was going with this.

Kurt exhaled, impatient. "All along we've assumed it was the mother who left them with me." He moved closer. "What if their real father doesn't know where they are?" he asked, as Paige drew in a halting breath and flattened her hands against his chest. What if all he had done here was let his ego get in the way of reuniting the real father with his baby daughters?

Paige empathized with him. "You're afraid you're going to give your heart to them, and then they'll be taken away."

Too late for that, Kurt thought sardonically. His heart was already involved. And, really ironically, with more than just the triplets.

That didn't mean he wasn't still duty-bound to do the right thing.

Still tingling from Paige's touch, he stepped away. Working to contain his disappointment, which seemed to get stronger with every minute that passed, he folded his arms and kept himself aloof. "I don't want to rob another person or family of children that rightfully belong with them."

Her brows drew together. She pushed the cloud of auburn hair from her face, ignoring his brooding look. "Don't you think if the girls had family who cared about them, a missing persons report would have been filed by now, an Amber Alert put out?"

"Sure, if their dad knows they exist." Kurt shrugged, quashing the urge to pull Paige close again and run his fingers through her hair. "It's possible their mother didn't tell the dad she was pregnant. What then?"

Paige fell silent, considering. Finally, she squared her shoulders, drew a breath and did exactly what he expected her to do when stressed. She tabled her emotions and went back to the preordained plan of dealing with this situation. "Well…" She raked her teeth across her lower lip. "Whatever the situation is, we'll find out tomorrow when Kyle contacts the state Bureau of Vital Statistics."

She drew a breath. "Once we get their information," she continued assuredly, "it shouldn't take law enforcement too long to track down the mother and or father listed on their birth certificates. By tomorrow night, the triplets could be back with their family. Or...paperwork signed so they can be placed elsewhere. We should be happy about finding a resolution to this situation," Paige finished, spreading her delicate hands, "whatever it is."

That was the problem, Kurt thought.

He wasn't happy.

And that infuriated him. He was the kind of guy who lived in the moment and led with his common sense and experience, not his heart. But right now, his feelings—for the kids and for Paige—were all he could think about. Even if he was beginning to see that this situation was probably not going to last more than another few days, if that, he wanted it to continue indefinitely. And honest to Pete, how stupid was that?

These kids weren't his, any more than Paige was his wife. It didn't matter *what* it felt like, or what illusions he had allowed himself to operate under for the last fifty-five hours.

The note, the babies being left on his doorstep were all probably destined to be as fleeting as Paige stepping into his life.

And yet stranger things had happened....

Could happen, if he was willing to let go of his doubts and expectations, and seduce her into letting go of hers....

But really, he thought wearily, how likely was that?

"We also have a meeting back in Laramie at noon tomorrow," Paige stated, her bossy, excessively organized side emerging once again.

Reminded of how it had been when they were kids, when she always seemed to be at least a half step ahead of him, going to great lengths to turn his life upside down, Kurt growled succinctly, "Your point?"

She looked at him like a crew boss tossing out orders to the hired hands. "We have a three-hour drive home tomorrow morning. We just got the triplets down for what we *think* is the night. We both should be getting some sleep."

Kurt knew Paige meant well.

That didn't mean what she was suggesting was even possible. Especially when all their little tête-à-tête had done was make him wonder what she had on beneath those flannel pajamas, if anything, and think about getting close to her once again.

"There's only one thing that will get me in that bed," he told her gruffly, figuring she had to be smart enough to let his bad mood chase her away. "So unless you're offering—" he paused significantly, making sure she got it "—you'll have to get some shut-eye alone."

Chapter Nine

Paige knew that Kurt was giving her attitude, the way he had when they were young. But she now knew the needling was just a ploy to keep her from getting too close. It wasn't who he was, and solitude was the last thing he needed. Determined to be there for him tonight, she clasped both his forearms and tipped her head up to his. "Then I'm offering," she said quietly.

Disbelief warred with the cynicism in his eyes. He was hurting, and that hurt drove him to keep her from furthering the fast-growing intimacy between them. His lip curled as he stated, "You're not up for flings, remember?"

Normally, Paige admitted, that was true. She wasn't. But it wasn't like she was surrendering to his considerable charms, either. She was doing this of her own volition.

She held his challenging gaze. "This is different."

His eyes tracked the pulse in her throat, the soft swell of her breasts, before returning ever so slowly and deliberately to her face. "Why?"

His voice was like velvet, it sent a shiver coursing over her skin. Paige swallowed around the sudden knot of emotion in her throat. "Because I know what it's like to have the possibility of a baby in your life." To be so full of joy and life and hope and the promise of a family to call your own. "And then have that baby taken away, just as suddenly as it was gifted," she finished sadly.

Briefly, a mixture of compassion and understanding lit his eyes. "Your miscarriage."

Paige splayed her hands across the solid musculature of his chest. Beneath his shirt, she felt the warmth of his skin, the strong, steady beating of his heart. "It took me years to get over it, Kurt." Years to feel she could go on. "Years to reconcile the fact that what I wanted was not what my baby's father desired...."

Kurt caught her hands in his, stopping the caressing movements of her fingertips. He looked down at her, holding her captive. "Is that why you're so determined to go it alone this time, be a single parent from the get-go, and content yourself with just the occasional whatever-this-is-to-you?" Kurt asked.

With her body tensing, Paige wrested her hands from his confining grip. She wound her arms about his shoulders and offered her lips up to his. "I don't care what this is. I don't want to quantify it. All I know for sure is that I want more than just one time with you, Kurt. And unless I'm wrong, you want more than that from me."

It wasn't the full-out surrender Kurt was looking for, but for the moment, it was close enough. Because Paige was right, he thought, as he gathered her close and buried his hands in the shiny, tousled layers of her auburn hair. He did need comforting. And there was nothing that felt better than the softness of her body against his. Nothing that satisfied better than the press of her lips, or the silky warmth of her tongue as it tangled with his. She was all woman. Contradictory, to be sure. But sweet and sexy, loving and tender. He needed someone like her in his life. He needed someone to help him sort out the mess he found himself in. Paige was direct enough, and close enough to the situation herself, to help him do that. And she was as in need of an injection of passion and excitement as he. So why shouldn't they just take it as it came? Make love because they felt like it? Coming together like this would push aside the ambivalence and confusion. Help them stop worrying, and wondering what was coming next, and just be in the here and now.

And right now, all he wanted was to feel the soft invitation that was Paige. She smelled like soap and the citrus blend of her shampoo. And tasted like woman and mint. And beckoned like a sweet, warm, feminine oasis. Needing to possess her the way no one else ever had, he lowered his head and nuzzled her neck, kissing and caressing until she whimpered and he felt her knees tremble. His blood rushed as she swayed against him, her fingers curling into his shoulders, urging him on. Satisfaction roared through him, coupled with a fierce driving need for more. Determinedly, he brought her flush against him, kissing her with everything he possessed inside.

Her body heating, she kissed him back just as passionately, her nipples beading against his chest. He let his palms slide down to the small of her back, and she responded with such aching vulnerability that he smiled in triumph. Unable to resist any longer he slid her pajama pants, and her thong, down and off.

Loving the way she felt, so warm and womanly, he

eased her legs apart. Caressed and explored the flatness of her abdomen, the insides of her thighs, the petal softness between. Knowing he'd never get enough of her, no matter how many times they made love, he kissed her over and over, until she was moaning and moving against him and the dampness flowed. Yearning to be closer yet, his need to be inside her as overwhelming as it was inevitable, he danced her backward toward the opened sofa bed. With his own body throbbing, desire thundering through him in waves, he eased his palm beneath her pajama top, under the silky camisole. Wanting to remember every moment of this night, he let his glance sift slowly over her as he traced the upper slope of her breast. And when those garments were off, too, she made a low sound of pleasure and arched her spine, giving herself over to the loving motions of his lips and hands.

Paige had thought she could separate the physical from the emotional. As it turned out, she couldn't. Making love with Kurt, sharing the care of the babies with him, had changed everything. She could not be with him now without seeing him in an entirely new light. Or wanting to be with him as equals. Friends. Co-parents. And most of all, like this…

Her pulse fluttering with excitement, she stripped off his loose cotton pajama pants, briefs and T-shirt. He was every bit as beautiful as she remembered. All hot, hard, demanding male. She pushed him down onto the sofa bed, cupped him with her hands and made him want. She kissed him like there was no tomorrow, until what few inhibitions remained between them dissolved. Her heart racing, she draped herself over him, letting him know what it was like to be the recipient of her sensual give and take. He groaned as she dipped her tongue into his navel, slid her hands over his hips, lifted him to her until his body took on an insistent throbbing all of its own.

And then they were shifting positions once again.

Her wrists were in his hand. He was lying on top of her, gently parting her thighs, possessing her sweetly. Just that swiftly, the pinnacle that had eluded her came, taking them both by surprise. Kurt chuckled in triumph, held her until the sensation passed, and then continued his possession once again.

Oh no! Paige thought. *I couldn't possibly...*

Kurt showed her she could. He took her to impossible heights, making her need as never before, until desire streamed through her like fire, and she rocketed with him to the outer limits of their control. They shuddered together in dizzying release, forging a connection unlike anything she had ever known. And suddenly Paige knew romance wasn't just a theory, a hope or a dream. It was real. It was here. It was all for the taking. It was Kurt.

"THAT WAS...SOMETHING," Kurt murmured, when at last they could breathe again. He lay on his back, one hand wrapped around her shoulder, the other folded behind his head.

Paige cuddled against him, her head nestled in the curve of his neck, her thigh draped over his. "Wasn't it...?" she whispered back.

He clasped her shoulders. All these years, he had relished his independence, never guessing he could want like this, feel like this. Determined to make this affair last, to make their lovemaking so satisfying and amazing she would never want to be with anyone else again, he pressed a kiss on her brow. Rolled so he could see her, and asked, "No regrets this time?"

She shook her head and kissed the curve of his shoulder. She looked spectacular, lying back against the sheets, her body all aglow. "None. Except..." She flashed him a breezy smile.

Here it came...

She continued shyly. "I wish we'd become friends a whole lot sooner."

"Friends" was not exactly what Kurt was aiming for, but he figured it was better than the rivals they had been to each other.

They would just have to build on that. And see where their relationship went from here. In the meantime, he only had one thing on his mind: making love to her again. Even more thoroughly this time...

She smiled, seeing the intent in his eyes. "You read my mind," she whispered, opening her arms to him again.

And that was the last either of them said for a very long time.

Paige and Kurt woke hours later to the sleepy murmurs of the triplets. From that moment on it was a marathon of activity, as they took care of the babies, packed up, checked out of the hotel and drove back to Laramie for their meeting with Mitzy Martin at social services.

Fortunately, they made it on time.

It was Kurt's brother who wasn't there when they arrived.

"Kyle called. He's going to be a few minutes late,"

Mitzy said, as she ushered them into her office. Still holding the door, she gave Kurt a questioning look. "He mentioned the two of you tracked down Camila Albright last night, in Dallas."

Kurt nodded, wishing he had better news to relay. He carried in two of the infants, still strapped in their car seats. Paige brought in the third. Carefully, they sat the babies down side by side. When they were satisfied the girls were still asleep, and not likely to wake, Kurt brought Mitzy up to date on his meeting with Camila.

"So the triplets are definitely not yours. And you have no idea who their parents might be?" the social worker said, looking as dejected about that as Kurt and Paige had both felt the evening before.

He could not completely contain his frustration. "None."

"Well, I guess that leaves you off the hook then," Mitzy said.

The practical part of Kurt wished he could just walk away. It would make his life—and the situation—so much simpler. The honorable part of him knew better....

"Not really, given the fact that Lindsay, Lori and Lucille were left specifically for me."

Paige added, "I know it's just been a few days, but we both feel a real responsibility for these children."

"I can see that," Mitzy stated gently. But Kurt could tell she was about to take them away, anyway.

Before she could do that, Kyle strode in.

Ready for some more definitive answers, Kurt turned to his brother. "What did you find out?"

He grimaced. "Nothing, unfortunately. The state

Bureau of Vital Statistics has no birth certificate on record for the triplets."

"So they weren't born in Texas?" Kurt surmised, cursing silently at this latest twist.

Mitzy lifted a hand and cut in. "Just because the department has received a birth certificate doesn't mean it's in the system. If there is something off—say the babies weren't named when they left the hospital, or the forms filed by the hospital or doctor don't match up precisely with the information given by the parent—the request for filing will be set aside until someone has a chance to personally correct the error. So their birth certificates could very well be sitting in a pile on someone's desk, awaiting correction or verification and processing."

Paige shot Kyle a troubled look. "So how long is it going to take before we find out whether that's the case or not? And if not, move the search elsewhere?"

Used to dealing with the often slow pace of bureaucracy, he shrugged. "It could be today. It could be a week. They're not sure. All they do know is that with Thanksgiving coming up, and several people out on vacation, they are very understaffed."

"Can't we do anything to speed it up?" Kurt asked in frustration.

"You can't," his brother told him. "You still have no legal right to the information, because of the privacy laws. But I can go down to Austin tomorrow as a law enforcement officer and see what I can do to speed up the process. And I plan to do just that."

"In the meantime," Mitzy interjected, taking charge of the meeting once again, "we need to talk about what's going to happen to the triplets next."

PAIGE KNEW FROM THE LOOK on her friend's face that the news wasn't good.

"We still can't find another foster home that can accommodate all three girls at once, so..."

"I can continue to foster them for a little bit longer," Paige volunteered.

Mitzy did a double take. Paige knew what her friend was thinking. She had done a complete one-eighty from where she'd been on Friday, when she'd been drafted for this assignment.

"What about your personal plans for the upcoming weekend?" Mitzy asked.

Flushing in embarrassment, Paige answered in a code only her best friend and Kurt would understand. "I'm still on for Saturday," she said. And would be as long as the situation with the triplets was resolved by then. If not, a new plan would have to be made. "That won't affect what I do in the meantime."

Out of the corner of her eye, Paige saw Kurt studying her, an inscrutable expression on his face.

"You also have to go back to work at the hospital, don't you?" Mitzy reminded her.

Technically, yes. But she'd gone the whole calendar year without taking any time off. There were other surgeons in the area who could fill in. "I have vacation coming," Paige said, her innate stubbornness kicking in. "I'll make arrangements."

Looking happy about that, Kurt moved closer to her in a show of solidarity. "I will, too."

Mitzy studied them both, a question in her eyes that seemed to encompass more than the children's welfare. "You're both going to continue to take time off," she repeated, as if she couldn't possibly have heard correctly.

Kurt shrugged and laced a companionable arm about Paige's shoulders, reminding her just how tenderly he had made love to her the evening before, when they both had been reeling from the news that he was not the triplets' biological daddy.

The closeness had helped her believe that happily-ever-afters still existed and would somehow happen for the three little girls. How could it not, with Kurt and the McCabe clan looking out for them? And, Paige reasoned, they had her and Mitzy, too. The two of them were no slouches when it came to looking out for the best interests of children.

"We're just talking about a few more days," Kurt said.

Feeling emboldened by his touch, Paige pointed out, "Thanksgiving is Thursday. We're both going to be off then, anyway." She looked at him, aware they'd yet to discuss plans for the holiday, and maybe should have before coming to the office today. "Right?"

He tilted his head to one side. Grimaced. "Yes and no. I'm on emergency call," he admitted.

Now that Paige thought about it… She sighed and raked her fingers through her hair. "So am I."

"But my parents will be back by then," Kurt interjected.

Paige smiled, triumphant. "And mine will be around, too."

"Plus all my siblings." Kurt continued persuading their case. "So we'll have plenty of backup for the kids if we need help caring for them."

Mitzy rocked back in her chair, still skeptical.

"I know you have a job to do here, Mitzy. I respect that," Paige said, shamelessly playing the friendship card. "But it'd be wrong to separate them for the holidays. Especially since this is their very first Thanksgiving."

"And where better to spend it than at the big bash Paige's parents always host?" Kurt added, helpful as ever when it came to the kids.

Mitzy tapped her pen against her desk, giving Paige a searching look. "Okay, but this is only until next Monday. We have a court date then. And the family court judge is going to want to see them in more permanent living arrangements."

"Thanks for helping me keep things status quo," Kurt said as he and Paige left the Laramie County Social Services office and walked out to the car, sleeping infants in hand.

"I did it as much for me as for you," she admitted.

He settled Lindsay's and Lucille's car seats into their bases. On the other side of the car, Paige fit Lori's seat in securely, too.

She straightened, to see him looking at her over the top of her station wagon. She didn't have to tell him how emotionally attached she had become to the three little girls; she knew he felt exactly the same way. "I need to know they're okay," Paige confided. "So until they are reunited with family or have a permanent place to go that offers everything they need, I'd like to keep them with me."

Kurt looked shocked. "As their foster mother?"

"Actually..." Paige inhaled deeply and forced herself to tell Kurt the truth. "I'm beginning to think about the possibility of adopting them on my own, in lieu of having a baby the new-fashioned way. I just haven't made a decision yet...and I won't. Not until this situation is settled."

Hurt flashed briefly in his blue eyes. Rather than be relieved to be absolved of the responsibility, he looked as if he felt almost...excluded.

Guilt flashed through her. She had been trying to help him out here, not hurt him.

Kurt narrowed his eyes and asked, "Is that because you think I won't adopt them? Since we know now they aren't my biological children?"

That assumption was why he had initially become so involved.

Her heart kicking against her ribs, Paige studied him with the same careful deliberation. "Would you?" Or would the lack of blood ties eventually end his culpability and his interest?

Kurt shrugged, his manner as offhand as hers was precise. "We don't yet know the reasons they were left with me, but I'm willing to take on the responsibility for them because it's the honorable thing to do."

And the McCabes were chivalrous men above all else, Paige knew.

"But that doesn't mean I want to take on all that alone," Kurt continued, even more sagely.

She resisted the urge to roll her eyes. Here came the kicker she'd been expecting. "Well, I guess that's the difference between us," she told him, feeling a little disappointed by the conditional stipulation of his aid. Not only would she give up her chance to have a biological child of her own, she'd change her life completely to accommodate the triplets. Hire nannies. Cut back her work schedule. In short, do whatever it took to make everything work the way it should. "Because I do want to take on the responsibility alone." She would happily be a single mom.

Kurt frowned. He came toward her and continued sensibly, "I thought we had already established that caring for the three of them is too much for any one person to handle. It's going to take two parents to bring them up."

Paige pushed away the romantic fantasy his words evoked. The little cocoon they had made for the five of them, while they were living at his parents' ranch, was not reality and never would be. She relied on black humor to bring them swiftly back to earth. "Whoever their mother is and you?" she corrected drily.

Kurt sent her a quelling look. "Me and whoever else wants to be involved. Whether that's their biological mother, and you and me...I don't know."

A bolt of jealousy shot through her. "You really think a *triangle* could work?" she asked in astonishment.

Kurt circled around the car to stand next to her. He flashed her a sexy grin and captured both her hands in his. "These three little girls brought us together in no time flat. And whoever would have thought that could happen?"

Not me.

Probably not anyone who knew us both, Paige thought, recalling the way she and Kurt had bickered about the plumbing repairs just days before.

Sensing a chink in her emotional armor, Kurt tucked a hand beneath her chin and continued even more persuasively, "The point is, Lucille, Lori and Lindsay need love. Lots of it. We both want to be involved in caring for them. And the five of us have made a pretty good family so far."

A wonderful little family, in fact. Fighting the tender feeling of well-being his touch generated, Paige pushed back with the reverse argument. "It's only been four days."

"Yeah." Kurt lifted her hand and pressed a kiss to the inside of her wrist. "And look how we've bonded."

That was the problem, Paige thought, wishing she wasn't so stirred by his sweet caress. Much more of this *bonding* and she'd be falling head over heels in love with a guy who might not be hers for the taking.

Impatient, she extricated herself from his grasp. "That could all be washed away in an instant if another woman enters the mix."

Kurt sobered with breathtaking speed. "Only if we let it. I'm perfectly willing to accept the responsibility given me here, Paige." He caught her hand again and gave it a squeeze. "I don't want to be with another woman. The only woman I want to be with is you."

She looked down at their entwined fingers and worked to slow her racing pulse. Finally, she asked, "What are you suggesting?"

"That we keep to our current arrangement," Kurt said, holding her gaze as if his solution was the most logical answer in the world. "I'll be the dad. You'll be the mom. And the three little girls will belong with both of us."

Chapter Ten

Kurt couldn't have stunned Paige more if he'd stripped naked in the center of the parking lot. Which in a sense, he admitted wryly, he had just done. At least on an emotional level...

Paige backed up another step and folded her arms, like a schoolmarm presiding over an unruly group of children. "We're not married."

"And we've proved we don't have to be to parent the girls effectively." Given Paige's excessively independent nature, he realized that letting her keep all her options open was probably the only way he could talk her into continuing their current arrangement. And he *wanted* it to continue....

"So why change anything—whether we still foster or eventually adopt? Why screw up something that's working? Especially if, as it now appears, the girls are going to need a permanent set of parents who will love them the way they're meant to be loved."

Paige rocked forward on the toes of her suede boots. She slipped her hands in her pockets and tipped up her chin, her sculpted cheekbones glowing pink. "You mean this, don't you?" she whispered in a shocked voice.

"You really want to take on this responsibility, biology notwithstanding."

Kurt edged closer.

Damn, but she was beautiful in the golden autumn sunlight. Her auburn hair framed her face in soft, untamed waves. Her grey cashmere sweater hugged her torso, emphasizing the slenderness of her waist and the fullness of her breasts. Matching flannel trousers molded her slender waist, clung lovingly to her hips and long, sexy legs.

He brushed a strand of silky hair from her cheek and tucked it behind her ear. "If it looks like they're going to remain wards of the state, at least for a while, then I'll take whatever classes I need and become a foster parent, too."

He'd meant to reassure Paige. Instead, she looked more dismayed than ever. After biting her lower lip, she warned in a low, wary voice, "There's more to it than that, Kurt. Home studies, applications, fees, court appearances..."

She seemed to think he didn't have it in him to do all that.

Irritated that she was letting her old impression of him impact her view of him now, he stroked both his hands through the mussed strands of her hair. "Then we'll do it step by step," he promised, looking deep into her eyes. "In the meantime, you'd keep your place, I'd keep mine. We'd hire a sitter or two to help us out, so we can go back to work. The girls could continue to stay with whichever one of us is free. But of course," he added hurriedly, "whenever we all wanted to be together, we could do that, too."

It would all be up to her. Whatever he had to do to keep her—and the girls—in his life, he would do.

The vulnerability and hesitation in her eyes began to fade. Her breath soughed out in a soft laugh. "Sell me on the idea, why don't you?"

He welcomed her wry teasing. It meant she was recovering her equilibrium. "You know what I mean."

Paige did know, Kurt noted. And she had no valid argument why his suggestion wouldn't work just fine.

Which was, he realized, the problem...in her view.

She wasn't ready to join forces with him permanently. Not in friendship, not in bed, not for the sake of the kids.

Determined to do what was right for all of them, he continued pushing for what he wanted. "Naturally, we can't stay at my parents' ranch forever."

An amused glimmer lit her green eyes. "Naturally not."

"But we live in the same neighborhood in Laramie. So as soon as my plumbing is fixed, too—"

Paige lifted a palm, halting him in midsentence. "What are you talking about?" she demanded. "Your plumbing is getting done first!"

Realizing his verbal slip, Kurt swore silently to himself.

Paige paused. Stepping closer, she propped her hands on her hips and peered at him through a fringe of thick auburn lashes. *"Isn't it?"*

Kurt shrugged. So much for his attempt at gallantry where she was concerned. "I meant for that to be a surprise," he told her reluctantly.

He had intended to impress her.

Instead, all he had apparently done was throw her off her guard once again.

"Now you've really confused me," Paige said ten minutes later, when they stopped by her home to see how the work was coming. Instead of just Rowdy and his assistant, there was a crew of ten guys working to replace all the pipe in the house. Which was not an easy job, since it required several walls being opened up so they could get at the plumbing lines. Walls which would then have to be repaired and repainted by the subcontractor Rowdy had hired to help with that.

"Yeah," Rowdy concurred genially. "Surprised me, too, when Kurt called first thing Saturday and asked if I could get some guys together to work all weekend. He didn't care that I had to get 'em from San Angelo and pay travel all the way here and back every day. That, plus the time-and-a-half for weekends, substantially added to the final cost."

Paige stepped back onto the porch, to get away from all the noise. Rowdy came with her. "But not to worry," the plumber rushed to reassure her. "The extra cost is not on your bill. It's on his."

Kurt walked up to join them. He stood in full view of the car, where the girls were sleeping peacefully in their car seats.

It was clear, Paige noted, that he had overheard enough to be embarrassed by the revelation of his unprecedented kindness.

He regarded her with a typically cool glance, then shrugged and muttered, "I figured I owed you for helping out with the triplets. Getting your house fixed before the Thanksgiving holiday, like you wanted, was the least I could do."

She was touched by his generosity. "Thank you."

"If I didn't know better, I'd say you cast some sort of spell on the guy," Rowdy stated, elbowing Kurt. "Or maybe it's just the three babies that have softened him up." He surveyed them both. "How's that working out for you-all?"

"Fine," Kurt said.

At the same time, Paige murmured, "Good."

"Hmm." Their pal grinned as the pounding, clanging and soldering continued. "Well, I'll be darned. Are the two of you...friends now?"

Were they friends? Or just co-baby-caretakers and occasional lovers? And where was the distraction of the triplets when they needed them? Paige wondered.

"Looks like," Kurt murmured evasively, already heading back to the station wagon to stand guard over their tiny charges.

Perplexed and hurt that he hadn't declared his affection for her a little more plainly, Paige went back in the house to get a closer look at the work going on, and gather up a few more of her things.

"So what is this?" she asked Kurt minutes later as she loaded another batch of clean clothes in the station wagon to take out to the ranch. She knew she was being pushy, but needed him to give her a clue. "Another if-it-feels-good-do-it moment for you?"

"Maybe an if-it-feels-right moment," he corrected. "You have to admit the triplets have brought us together in a way neither of us could have foreseen. We make a good team. And the kids seem to like us, too."

Paige couldn't argue with that. "What's not to like? We cater to their every need."

"But...?" He studied the mixture of indecision and disappointment on her face.

"Feminine instinct tells me you'll still be in the picture at the end of the day. I'm not so certain I will. Particularly if there's another woman with a big-time crush on you involved."

"It wouldn't matter if there was."

"You say that now. But you haven't come face-to-face with her yet. You don't know who she is. And unless one of us finds a way to speed up identifying said woman in a manner that doesn't involve breaking the medical privacy laws, we're kind of stuck, waiting around." *With me falling deeper and deeper in lust with you every day.*

Which was a disaster, since the last thing Paige wanted was to fall into another crisis-driven romance as she had during her first year in med school.

She was smarter now. Older, wiser. But in some ways just as scared of failure, and just as vulnerable and in need of love, support and understanding, as she had been then.

The problem was, that type of connection was based on the circumstances of the crisis itself. She had learned the hard way how a relationship like that did not hold up in the demands of the real world.

And for her to lose Kurt the way she had lost Neil...

Because their relationship was based on all the wrong

things and could not hold up to the stress of unexpected events—or real-life disappointment…

She'd be devastated. Truly devastated.

Kurt shrugged. "We could still go to the press."

"Given the kind of media circus that would likely create, I still think it's a bad idea."

"So do I…"

Kurt looked down at the kids. Lucille had worked both arms out from under the blanket covering her. As she sleepily waved them about, he focused on the gold ID bracelet gleaming on her tiny wrist.

He turned back to Paige, who smiled as the next idea hit them simultaneously.

"Are you thinking what I'm thinking?" he asked with a grin.

"It would appear that I am," she said. She just didn't know why it hadn't occurred to them sooner.

"WHO WOULD HAVE THOUGHT there'd be over ninety-two thousand internet sites in Texas alone for baby ID bracelets?" Paige wondered aloud several hours later.

She and Kurt had been taking turns, searching the web for a bracelet identical to those the three girls were wearing. And thus far had come up with nothing.

"Not to mention ones with bells and birds and flowers, in variations of sterling silver, stainless steel and eighteen carat gold?"

They sat together on the sofa, their bodies touching from shoulder to knee. "Do you think we're wasting our time?" Paige asked finally.

Kurt scowled. "Possibly."

They both fell silent, thinking deeply.

He studied the bracelet they had temporarily removed from Lucille's wrist. "Maybe we're just using the wrong approach." He traced the filigreed design along the edges of the nameplate, the unique braiding of the chain. "These bracelets are really nice."

"They certainly feel and look expensive." Paige paused. "Maybe we should just start with a list of the top jewelers in Texas and conduct our search that way."

Kurt snapped his fingers. "Or the organization that serves them all."

He typed in a search for Texas Jewelers Association. "Let's call them and see if they can help us."

Three phone calls later, Kurt was speaking with the president of the TJA. A very nice man, he agreed to do what he could to help identify the store that had sold the baby ID bracelets.

"Although the actual sales data will still remain private," he told them, "the store owners can certainly tell us if they carry that particular item, and get back to you with at least some preliminary information as to cost, how long they've been carrying the design, whether it's unique to them and so forth."

"How long do you think it will take to get a response?" Paige asked.

"I'll send out a mass emailing this evening," the organization president promised. "So hopefully, in the next day or so, you'll be contacted by the appropriate merchant."

Relieved, Kurt and Paige thanked him and hung up. "Now what?" she asked.

No sooner had she spoken than the sleeping triplets began to stir. Lindsay let out a hungry wail, swiftly echoed by Lucille and Lori.

Kurt grinned and stood up, holding out his hand. "I think our little darlings just told us.…"

"I'M WRITING IT DOWN NOW, Mom," Paige told her mother over the phone several hours later.

Walking away from the living room, where the babies had just gone to sleep in the buggy, she grabbed a piece of paper from the kitchen counter and started scribbling. "A triple batch of cranberry compote—or enough to serve approximately thirty-six."

The annual multifamily Thanksgiving dinner had grown over the years. The celebration now included approximately two hundred and fifty members of the Lockhart, McCabe, Carrigan and Chamberlain clans, along with their guests. It had grown so large that it was held on one of the soundstages on her father's Laramie, Texas, movie studio.

"We plan to eat at three o'clock. It would be nice if the food could be there at least an hour before."

Paige smiled, already looking forward to the holiday. As always, there was much to be thankful for in her life. "No problem."

"Kurt can go in with you on the compote."

That made it sound as if they were an official couple.

Fearing it was tempting fate at this point to make that leap, Paige interjected, "Are you sure? Doesn't he usually show up with soft drinks or something?"

"Yes."

Her mother was clearly in organizer mode. Paige could hear typing on the other end.

"But since Annie McCabe and I assumed you would be coming together with the three babies," Dani continued crisply, "we decided to count you as one unit this year."

In the family room, Paige heard the beginning of a wail.

As had been happening all evening, every time they got the girls to sleep, and put them down, one of them woke. The first time it had been Lucille fretting and jostling her two sisters. The next time it was Lori. Paige wasn't sure, but she thought this time it sounded like Lindsay doing the fussing.

"Everything okay there?" Dani asked with concern.

"Yes. They're just restless tonight, that's all."

"I'll let you go then, honey. And Paige—call if you need anything."

"I will, Mom. Thanks." She severed the connection and put her phone down. She went into the family room, where a perplexed Kurt was standing over the buggy, gently rolling the wheeled carriage back and forth. Usually, the motion lulled them back to sleep. Tonight the gentle rocking only infuriated them and increased their wailing. All three babies were now waving their fists, kicking and howling with increasing ferocity.

His blue eyes darkened with worry. "Do you think they might be getting sick or something?"

Good question, and one that Paige had just been considering herself. "Let me get my medical bag. It wouldn't hurt to check their ears."

While Kurt wheeled the babies into the bedroom and lifted them out onto the guest bed, she got out the otoscope. With his assistance, she managed to check all three sets of ears, throats and noses. She pulled out her stethoscope and checked their hearts and lungs. "Everything is fine there," she murmured.

Then for good measure, even though she was certain what the answer was going to be, she took their temperatures. "Perfectly normal."

"So they're not sick," Kurt deduced.

Paige sat on the left side of the bed. Kurt sat on the right. All three babies were lined up between them, side by side.

And now that their temper tantrums were over, the infants were lying quietly, looking at each other and cooing. To the point that Kurt and Paige couldn't help but chuckle.

"Well, now that they worried us sick, I guess the storm has passed," he drawled.

Paige studied the three girls, looked over at the enormous English-style pram, then back at them. "Do you think the buggy might be getting too small for them to sleep in?"

Kurt considered that. "Maybe."

"Think we ought to mix it up a little and try putting them in a crib?" she asked.

He ran a hand beneath his jaw. "Actually, we probably should have done that a lot sooner."

Paige wrinkled her nose. "We had our reasons for not wanting to mess with the status quo."

"Live and learn." He stood up. "Let me call my mom

in California and see where she keeps the port-a-cribs the other grandkids use...."

Half an hour later, they had located two mesh-sided port-a-cribs and the soft cotton sheets that went with them. Kurt set the first crib up in the bedroom where the triplets had been sleeping during the night. Paige stopped him before he could open up the other. "Do you think we should separate them, so they won't keep waking each other up?" she asked, her hand on the baby buggy, where the third one was going to reside, alone this time.

As always, she was one step ahead of him in the organization department. "Probably a good plan," Kurt said, surprised that he didn't really mind sharing ideas with her tonight. Usually, he liked to call the shots. And that went double where Paige Chamberlain was concerned.

She edged closer. "How about one in my room, one in yours and the third in the guest room in between?"

"Hear that, girls?" Kurt teased, inhaling the enticing scent of the woman who was fast taking over his life. "You're going to chaperone tonight!"

Paige blushed the way she did when he was about to kiss her. She stepped back, as if just now realizing how much fun this was going to be. "Okay, *Daddy,* that's enough of that," she reprimanded with a facetiously stern look.

Kurt chuckled.

Ten minutes later, they had all the sleeping places set up.

They changed diapers, fed the triplets another few ounces or so of formula, burped them and rocked them to sleep. Finally, all three were gently snoozing once again.

Ever so quietly, Kurt and Paige settled them in their new quarters.

Tiptoed back out.

They were halfway down the hall when yet another howl erupted. Then a second, and a third.

They went back to rocking, got the girls to sleep, put them down. Only to have them start wailing again, even more furiously this time.

Throughout the rest of the evening, it didn't matter how they tried—or what they did—they could not get the girls to settle down separately.

Yet the moment they brought them all back together on the bed, and the babies could see each other, they relaxed again. Kicked, cooed and smiled, and finally, with a lot of awkward flailing around, managed to link hands.

"They may be too big to fit comfortably in the baby buggy," Paige murmured, "but they need to see each other to feel secure."

"Makes sense, if you think about it," Kurt answered. "They've been together from the time they were in the womb. Been separated from their mommy—or whoever was taking care of them from the time they were born—till now. No wonder they want to hang on to each other. Anything else at this point would be just too traumatizing."

Paige studied the way the babies were touching each other, making sure they were all together and all doing fine. The sweetness of the gesture brought a lump to her throat and an ache to her heart.

She caught Kurt's glance. "I don't know how this is all going to work out in the end, but I know this," she said, her lower lip quivering. "We can't let them be separated, Kurt."

He wrapped her in his arms and held her tight. "That won't happen. I won't let it, I promise you," he said thickly, meaning it from the bottom of his heart. "We'll do whatever we have to do to keep them together, as a family."

And while he was at it, he'd make sure that he and Paige stayed part of their lives.

Chapter Eleven

"Something smells great in here," Kurt said when he returned late on Wednesday from an afternoon of running errands.

Thanks to the generosity of his three sisters-in-law, and a delivery made earlier in the day, Lindsay, Lori and Lucille were all settled happily in bouncy seats. Paige had lined up the triplets in the center of the big kitchen table, so the three infants could see everything she did, and keep her company while she cooked.

Paige suddenly felt like a stay-at-home mom whose very handsome husband had just come home from work. Happiness bubbled up inside her. "It's the cranberry compote." She gave the bubbling mixture another stir.

Kurt leaned down to give each of the girls a kiss, then ambled over to where Paige stood at the stove. He wrapped an arm around her waist with husbandly affection, hauled her close and pressed a light kiss on her brow. "Mmm," he breathed in a way that had her wondering if he was referring to her or the bubbling confection in the three big saucepans. "What's in it?"

Paige warmed at the sheer masculine appreciation in his blue eyes. Happy that she was cooking with her usual skill today, instead of her previous ineptness, she ticked off the list of ingredients. "Fresh cranberries. Sugar. Orange zest and orange. Chopped apple. Cinnamon. Ginger. And pecans." And not a mistake or an error in the whole process!

Kurt leaned over, inhaling the aromatic steam coming from the pot.

Noticing how well he filled out his jeans—and secretly wishing they could throw caution to the wind and make love again—Paige did her best to contain her rising emotions, and offered blithely, "You want to taste it?"

He flashed an avaricious grin. "Oh, yeah."

She plucked a spoon from the drawer and took a little from the top. Acutely aware of the arm he still had wrapped around her, she blew on the bubbling fruit. "You're going to have to be careful." She blew again. "It's really hot." Only when she was satisfied that it was cool enough did she lift the spoon to his lips.

He tasted it, then pantomimed going weak in the knees. "Wow," he said when he'd swallowed. "That is absolutely amazing."

Paige glowed with pride. "Don't get too excited. It's my mother's recipe."

His eyes sparkled all the more. "You should taste it."

Her heart leaped at his nearness. "I already have."

"Try it again." Playfully, he took the spoon from her and guided it to her lips. "You'll be amazed."

Paige shook her head in amusement and dutifully parted her lips. She knew it was her imagination, but she could swear she tasted Kurt's lips on the spoon. A fact that made the sweet dish even better.

She nodded as the flavor melted on her tongue. "Mmm." She squinched her features in a comical parody of thoughtfulness, then grinned. "That is good. Really good."

Finished, she reached over and turned off the burners. "Now all we have to do is let it cool, refrigerate it and voila...our contribution to the meal will be taken care of."

"I like the sound of that." Pulling her close again, he kissed her gently.

A thrill sifted through her.

She wished they *could* make love then and there.

Unfortunately...

Paige cast a glance over her shoulder. Saw three smiling faces. "We've got an audience."

Lazily, Kurt straightened. "And they have a brand-new bed to sleep in tonight...."

Paige blinked. "You were able to get a full-size crib?"

"The only question was—who to borrow it from. All three of my older brothers were eager to help out. They're pleased as punch to see me joining the ranks of the happily settled dads in the family."

He really did seem more settled, Paige thought. Amazingly so. And after only six days!

As if on cue, her cell phone began to ring. It had been going off all afternoon. "I better get that. It might be the hospital." She eased away from Kurt's arms and walked across the kitchen, feeling his eyes upon her.

"You still on call for tomorrow?"

"Yep," she replied, over her shoulder. On a whim, she tossed him a sexy look. "But I've got someone to cover for me the rest of the weekend."

Paige turned back to the telephone. Noting the caller ID, she tensed. She really should have taken care of this earlier.

She picked up, intending to talk about her options, and instead found herself listening to a prerecorded message instead of a live person.

"What's wrong?" Kurt asked when she'd hung up without saying anything more than hello.

Paige set her cell phone back on the charger. "That was the fertility clinic, reminding me that I need to get an injection of HCG on Friday to make me ovulate. Also, I still need to choose the donor sperm, and I have an appointment on Saturday to be artificially inseminated."

The information seemed to hit him like a sharp blow to the solar plexus. He lifted an eyebrow. "You're still doing that?"

A self-conscious warmth flooded Paige's cheeks. She lifted her shoulders in a shrug and turned her eyes away, hating the disappointment she saw on his handsome face. "I don't know," she murmured. Her emotions in turmoil, she walked over to the girls and kissed each of their waving fists in turn. She smiled as they gurgled happily in response and continued visually tracking her every move.

Paige sighed and turned back to Kurt. "At first there didn't seem to be a reason to change my appointment. Now…" She raked her teeth across her lip. "I'm thinking I should put it off for another month, until this situation is resolved."

"That might make sense," he said carefully.

Paige knew that.

He folded his arms over the hard muscles of his chest. "But you're not sure."

Paige met his steady, assessing gaze. Wanting him to understand, and not think less of her, she found herself confiding, "I had hoped to be pregnant by Christmas. Having a baby of my own was supposed to be my present to myself." The best in a very long time.

He shrugged and dropped his arms to his sides. "It sounds like a good one."

She swallowed around the sudden, parched feeling in her throat. *It would be.* "Being with the triplets, taking care of them, has only reinforced my desire to have a family of my own."

He nodded in understanding. "Mine, too."

Paige kept her eyes locked with his, continuing wryly, "Canceling my appointment almost feels like tempting fate. Likely the moment I do that, Lindsay, Lori and Lucille's mother is going to show up and tell us why the two of *you* should be together, bringing up the triplets." And then Paige would be out in the cold. Alone. Childless once again… With a flourishing career and no hope of marriage or a child of her own in sight.

Having a satisfying professional life was not enough to make her happy. She saw that now. She needed, wanted, more. She wanted Kurt and the girls…and the familial happiness that still seemed to be eluding her.

He came close enough to wrap his arms around her. "Even if that happened—and it does not seem likely, now that Camila is out of the picture—it doesn't mean I'd be interested."

His implacable tone said he would not join forces with another woman, but Paige had been disappointed before, by another man she'd believed cared deeply for her.

The warmth and strength of his body engulfed her, making it difficult to keep track of the argument she was trying to make. Harder still to fight the need for closeness. She drew a deep breath and tried again.

"You say that now," she argued back, "when it's just a theoretical question...."

He lowered his head and scored his thumb across her lower lip. "I'll say it if and when that happens, too."

Excitement soared through her. "You love those little girls, Kurt," Paige reminded him as he touched his lips to hers in an angel-soft kiss. She drew back reluctantly. "You feel a responsibility for them." One that went deeper than she ever could have imagined....

Retaining his possessive hold on her, he shrugged. "So do you," he pointed out.

Paige splayed her hands across the wall of his chest, not sure if she was trying to keep him at bay or increase their closeness. "I may be their foster mother, but you still seem more likely to end up with them."

Kurt smiled at her in the same indulgent way she had seen other men smile at their wives. "Unless we both end up with them," he murmured huskily.

Tangling his hands in her hair, he brought her close enough for a slow, tender kiss. "I only have one priority right now, Paige. And that is you and these three little girls." He kissed her again, passionately this time.

"I feel the same." She kissed him back, then met his eyes, sure now what she was going to do. "I can't call the clinic—it's already closed for the Thanksgiving holiday. But it is open on Friday. So…" Paige inhaled sharply, forcing herself to take the leap. "If nothing is changed, I'll call then. In the meantime—" she took a step back again "—have you heard from Kyle? Do you have any idea how his investigation is going?"

"WE WERE ABLE TO FIND ONE possibility late today," Kyle told them over the phone, when he finally returned their call several hours later. "A single mother in Houston had three girls on August 16. She didn't name the triplets while she was in the hospital, and attempts to follow up afterward to get the information were not successful. That's why the information wasn't officially entered into the BVS computer system yet, or the triplets' birth certificates issued."

"Is it possible she's the one?"

"I don't know. When we found this, we decided to stop looking further until I had time to check it out. Anyway, apparently this woman had the children by an in vitro fertilization procedure and sperm donor. So there is no father listed on the birth certificate, nor will there be one. But I have to find her to check out the rest of it, and see if her babies are still with her, or what the situation might be. As we speak, I'm headed to the last address listed for her, off Memorial Parkway. How's your search with the jewelers coming?" Kyle asked, all business. "Anything there?"

Kurt brought him up to date. "We've heard from a number of Texas Jeweler Association members saying they don't carry that particular infant ID bracelet. None claiming it yet. But they have hundreds of members, so we have a ways to go there."

"You'll let me know the minute you come up with something," Kyle said.

"Will do. And you promise to do the same," Kurt replied.

They all said goodbye. Kurt turned off the speakerphone. "Well, that was good news. Sort of," he told Paige. "At least we now have one solid lead."

To a single mom who somehow was acquainted with or knew of Kurt and his family, Paige thought. She didn't know why the idea that another woman would go to such lengths to ensure her children would be part of the wealthy McCabe clan should leave her feeling so unsettled. She just knew she suddenly felt a lot less secure....

Telling herself it was foolish to jump to conclusions, she forced herself to take a more optimistic view. "Maybe they'll all be reunited in time for Thanksgiving," she murmured. "Maybe this has all been the result of postpartum depression, or something else that can be remedied."

Kurt looked her straight in the eye. "You really think that could be the case?"

"I don't know," she admitted ruefully, forcing herself to be objective. "I can't imagine voluntarily abandoning Lindsay, Lori and Lucille on anyone's doorstep, if they were my babies."

"Nor can I."

"But I also know how important it is to be loved by your parents, or in this case, maybe one parent. So in that sense," Paige reasoned with professional aplomb, "it would be good for the girls to be reunited with the mommy who gave birth to them, and to grow up feeling secure in her love."

KURT WASN'T SURPRISED that Paige had taken the generous view. She had a heart as big as Texas. And now that he knew her better, he realized she was also a very empathetic, forgiving woman. That, plus her desire to help people in whatever way she could, made her a very good physician and an excellent foster mother.

He wished he could say he was as charitable and compassionate, but he wasn't sure that was the case. His gut instinct told him the triplets' mother had known exactly what she was doing when she'd left the babies on his parents' doorstep. This was no impetuous or ill-thought-out action. The move had been calculated to ensure that the three infants would be ensured a safe and happy future as members of the legendary Texas McCabe clan. As such, the three beautiful little girls would not want for love or money or attention. There would be no reason for the person who'd orphaned them to feel guilty. Hence, Kurt did not expect their mother to change her mind and want the girls back. He figured if she were going to have a change of heart, she would have already come back to collect them.

She hadn't.

So all that was left to do, Kurt reasoned, was take care of the legalities. Which was no small detail, given the circumstances they were in.

Plus he had to convince Paige that he was as serious about keeping her in his life as he was about keeping the triplets.

"IF I DIDN'T KNOW BETTER," Dani Chamberlain murmured to Paige the following day, after she and Kurt walked in to the Thanksgiving festivities with all three girls, "I'd think you were one big happy family."

Paige looked over at Kurt, who had an infant in each arm. He shrugged and smiled at her parents. "Feels like it to me, too," he murmured with his usual laid-back ease.

Beau Chamberlain squinted thoughtfully at him, then turned back to Paige with fatherly affection. He gave her a hug and kissed her forehead. "You look happier than I've seen you in a very long time, too."

Paige basked in her parents' obvious approval as she worked the crocheted cap from Lori's dark curls. "I really like being a mom," she admitted.

Dani gazed at her, her mother's intuition in full force. "Is that all it is? Or is there something more going on here between the two of you?"

Paige was still figuring out how to reply to that when Kurt answered, "We're friends."

"Friends," Dani repeated unhappily as Kurt's parents, who had just flown in from the West Coast, joined the group.

Paige wasn't exactly happy with Kurt's quick answer, either, for totally different reasons. She felt like a whole heck of a lot more than a friend to him.

It wasn't that she wanted their parents to know she and Kurt had hooked up. She didn't really want anyone else to know they'd made love. It was too private, too special…and way too romantic for her to share. Romantic enough for her to feel, deep down, that regardless of the things that hadn't yet been said, she was more than just his friend, and vice versa....

"Who are we talking about?" Annie McCabe asked, greeting everyone with Texas-style hugs.

Since Kurt had "rescued" her from her mother's inquisition, Paige figured it was her turn to jump in and save him. "Kurt was just telling my parents that we've gotten to know each other a lot better and realize we're not *quite* the mortal enemies we thought we were a week ago."

She relaxed as everyone laughed at her teasing gibe.

"Well, that's good to know." Annie smiled and gave her an extra hug. "I always thought if you two would stop squabbling long enough to talk to each other, you'd get along famously."

Paige's smile was beginning to feel as if it were stuck to her face. "Well, it's happened. All due to these little darlings." She indicated the infant in her arms and the two in Kurt's.

"Babies do have a way of bringing people together," Dani murmured even more thoughtfully. "Just like the holidays..."

"And speaking of coming together..." Annie glanced at the beehive of activity around them. Tables were being set up all over the soundstage, cloths smoothed, centerpieces brought out. "How are things going in the kitchen area? Does anyone know?"

Dani gave the baby in Paige's arms a last, loving look and a buss on the cheek. "I was just about to go find out."

"I could use a hand bringing in our contribution."
Beau looked directly at Kurt.

"No problem," Kurt said.

And Paige's heart sank.

Chapter Twelve

"I'm concerned about Paige," Beau announced as the two of them walked out to the parking lot.

Kurt braced himself for the inquisition slash lecture sure to come. Paige's father was not only the larger-than-life hero of the big-screen Western, he was also an Oscar-winning director who knew exactly what he wanted to see from each and every situation—on film, and in life. A perfectionist in his work, and famously down-to-earth in his personal life, he was used to calling the shots. And he was highly protective of the two women who comprised his family.

Beau stopped to collect two dolleys just inside a loading dock. He passed the handle of one to Kurt. "She's fallen in love with those babies."

So have I, Kurt thought. "Paige has been a godsend this past week," he told her dad.

To the point that he wasn't sure what they would have done without her. Certainly, the babies would have been split up. He'd have lost the chance to get to know them. And her…

"Paige deserves a family of her own," Beau countered with a serious glance.

Kurt had only to think about the tenderness and affection with which she cared for the triplets, the joy on her face whenever she held one in her arms, and the delight Lori, Lindsay and Lucille exhibited in return, to know what a wonderful mother she would be. "I agree," he told her father firmly.

Beau opened up the back of his Cadillac Escalade. Inside were half a dozen cases of Napa Valley wine, and an equal amount of sparkling grape juice. "Unfortunately, my daughter's innate need to take care of others keeps getting in the way of that."

Maybe not as much as you think, Kurt thought, recalling Paige's undisclosed plans to have a baby on her own, the new-fashioned way. Knowing he could not betray her confidence and tell her dad about that, he remained silent.

Clearly, a mistake. Beau seemed to know Kurt was withholding something.

"Her mother and I want Paige to be happy. We want her to be loved. We don't want her getting so wrapped up in other people's problems she forgets to pursue her own dreams."

And Paige's dream, Kurt knew, was to have a family of her very own.

"What did my father say to you?" Paige asked, minutes later, when she went out to her Volvo station wagon with him to bring in the three large containers of chilled cranberry compote.

Knowing the triplets were being well taken care of by their mothers, Kurt welcomed the rare moment alone with Paige. He slowed his pace to enjoy the sunlit

November afternoon and crisp fall weather as they made their way through the rows of vehicles to Paige's car.

"I know he said something, Kurt," Paige insisted, when he didn't answer right away. "When the two of you walked out that door, Dad had the same look on his face that he did when I was sixteen and brought boys home."

"And what kind of look was that?" Kurt teased, delaying the inevitable.

She lifted her chin, her eyes flashing defiantly. "The look that says no man on earth is ever going to be good enough for his only daughter!"

Kurt grinned. So despite all her protestations to the contrary, she thought they were a couple, too! Otherwise, she wouldn't be so worried about the two of them gaining her father's approval. Nor, for that matter, would he.

Kurt stopped in the shadow of a two-ton pickup truck. Obscured from view by the vehicle, he slipped his hand into Paige's. "Your dad knows you are a caretaker by nature. It's why you were always the first to volunteer as a kid, why you took those foster parenting classes... why you became a doctor. No one who knows you is surprised at how quickly you've bonded with the triplets." He paused to let his words sink in. "What would surprise them is how quickly you've become involved with me."

Paige looked horrified. The color drained from her face. "Tell me you didn't let on to my father that you and I..."

Kurt momentarily bristled at her outburst, but he

pushed aside his hurt feelings. "Of course not." He paused, letting the weight of his words sink in.

Realizing their privacy was guaranteed, she relaxed.

"But I wanted to." The need to possess her roaring through him, Kurt gripped her hand more tightly to pull her into his arms. He savored how beautiful she looked. "I want to tell the whole world how I feel about you. How important you've become to me," he whispered. And then he did what he'd been yearning to do all day. He held her close and kissed her.

PAIGE COULDN'T BELIEVE she and Kurt were making out in the parking lot of her father's movie studio in broad daylight.

But they were.

And she didn't care.

Not if it meant feeling this swept away...

She wreathed her arms around his neck and kissed him back with all the feeling she had pent up inside her. She kissed him as if she was falling in love with him. As if theirs wasn't a temporary passion at all, but something stronger, deeper, and a heck of a lot more long lasting.

And of course, that was when it happened.

The pager strapped to Kurt's waist began to emit that annoying on-call buzz.

Reluctantly, they moved apart.

He grimaced, whispered, "Sorry" and then answered the page. "Doc McCabe..." Obviously concerned, he listened. "Can you get Bowser to the vet clinic? Try to keep him as calm as possible. Five minutes. I'll be there, waiting. See you then." Kurt ended the call. "One of my patients has part of a turkey carcass wedged in his jaw."

"Oh, dear. Sounds painful."

"As well as potentially life-threatening..."

Paige hurried with Kurt to her station wagon. Quickly, they unloaded the three heavy containers of chilled cranberry compote and headed back toward the soundstage.

"How did that happen?" Paige asked.

He shook his head. Because his hands were full, he waited for her to hold the door. "No one's really sure."

Paige made a face. "Was it cooked?"

Arriving at the busy kitchen, Kurt set the containers down and reached for hers. "I sure hope so. Otherwise, it's going to be salmonella city for that rowdy Chesapeake retriever." He stopped and looked into her eyes.

Paige saw regret that he was leaving her and the triplets. And something else deeper and infinitely more satisfying. Something that said they weren't finished here, and wouldn't be for some time. "Save me a plate?" he asked quietly.

She nodded. "Hurry back." She brushed his cheek with her lips, not caring if the gesture was the kind a real wife would have made. He caught her to him, kissed her back—on the mouth—then headed out. Still smiling, Paige went to find the triplets.

KURT DID HURRY BACK. But when he got there, Paige had been called in to the hospital to take care of an emergency. By the time she returned, he had been summoned to minister to a parrot with a broken wing, and a kitten who'd escaped during the festivities, battled with a thorn bush and lost. And so it went for the rest of the day.

By the time the party broke up at six, Kurt was back and Paige was still at the hospital. Kurt's mother, who had been watching over the triplets in his absence, took one look at his face.

"Did you ever eat today?"

So much for their first Thanksgiving as a family, Kurt thought. If he and Paige and the babies hadn't spent the morning together, hanging out and getting ready for the party, they would barely have seen each other at all. But not wanting his mother to know how disappointed he was that he'd missed out on a holiday meal with Paige and the girls, he shrugged. "I grabbed a bite here and there."

"Mmm-hmm." Annie tilted her head the way she always did when she thought he wasn't taking proper care of himself. "What about Paige?"

Kurt shrugged and bussed the top of Lucille's head.

Observing, Lindsay reached out for him. Kurt handed off Lucille and picked up Lindsay. He kissed her, too, then answered his mother's query. "I have no idea whether Paige had a chance to eat much or not, since I've barely seen her."

Lori began kicking her feet. She lifted a tiny hand toward Kurt.

He handed Lindsay to Paige's mom, who had come up to join them. He took Lori from his mother and bussed the top of her head in turn.

"No," Dani said, "Paige didn't have a chance to eat, although I tried to get her to do so before she went off to the hospital that last time."

"When does her on-call end?" his mom asked.

"Seven tomorrow morning, same as mine," Kurt stated.

"Well, then, the babies should stay with your father and me," Annie said firmly. "You two can take over again tomorrow morning, if you get any sleep tonight. Judging by the activity so far today, you may not."

Kurt knew his mom thought he worked too hard. What she didn't understand was that hard work did more than fill up the hours and add to his bank account—it kept the loneliness at bay.

Acutely aware it was always going to be a two by two world, and thus far he'd pretty much been a table-for-one guy—until Paige and the babies came along, anyway— he smiled and reluctantly relinquished Lori to his dad. "That's just the way it is in the medical and veterinary professions, Mom. Holidays always bring lots of family chaos, and hence, lots of emergencies of all kinds."

"Be that as it may, you still need a breather after the week you've had, and I imagine so does Paige. And there's no sense in driving back out to our ranch this evening, only to have to drive all the way back into town. So...do the two of you have places to stay?"

Yes, Kurt thought. *And no.* He lifted a staying hand. "Not to worry, Mom. We'll figure something out."

PAIGE HAD JUST FINISHED talking to her young patient's parents about their daughter's emergency appendectomy when Kurt walked into the surgery waiting room. She finished reassuring them, accepted their thanks and then walked over to him. He looked as happy to see her as she was to see him.

"Hey," she said, resisting the urge to act like a teen-ager on a date and link hands with him.

He stuck his palms in his back pockets, rocked back on his heels and looked down at her, his blue eyes crinkling at the corners. "Hey back."

Surprised to see him alone, she asked, "Where are the babies?"

"With my folks. They have determined that we deserve a night off."

Paige's soft lips twisted ruefully. "If you can consider it that, since we're both still on call till morning."

Kurt chuckled. "Exactly the point my mom made. Anyway, she suggested we stay here in town, and let them do the diapers and bottles tonight while we concentrate on our work and get whatever rest we can."

Paige didn't argue; she knew it was the best course for all concerned. She fell into step beside him as they walked down the hall. "Any further word from Kyle?"

"I had a text a while ago that said he's still looking for the woman. Apparently, she packed up all her stuff early this week, but hasn't turned the keys over to the apartment management yet. She's supposed to do that tomorrow morning. So if she shows, he said he'll intercept her then."

Paige tensed. "And if she doesn't…"

Kurt shrugged. "He'll keep looking."

She pivoted to face him. "And in the meantime…"

"We wait," he said, reassuring her as best he could. "And try not to second-guess the situation." Silence fell. Conscious of how pretty she looked in her blue scrubs, and how much he wanted to take her in his arms, Kurt said, "So, are you done here?"

Paige's eyes lit up. "Actually, yes." She flashed a cheerful smile. "I want to talk to the nurses one more time, and change out of my scrubs, but then I can go."

"I'll wait for you in the lobby," he said with a nod.

Paige headed off quickly. "See you in ten."

KURT WAS RIGHT, Paige thought as she finished up the charts, talked to the nurses and slipped into the locker room. There was no point in borrowing trouble by worrying about what was going to happen next with the babies. Right now, they were loved and cared for. Mitzy Martin and the CPS would make sure that remained the case.

There were still a few hours of Thanksgiving left.

She was going to spend them with Kurt.

And hopefully, this time there would be no more interruptions to their holiday. "So where are we going?" Paige asked when she joined him in the hospital lobby.

"It was supposed to be a surprise with the girls..." Kurt drawled with a wink "...had the day worked out a little differently."

She raised her eyebrows.

"As it happens, it'll be just the two of us," he added mysteriously, "but the babies will be there in spirit."

Paige tucked her arm through his. "Now you've got me curious." She did a little happy dance and watched him grin all the more. "So where are we going?" She fell into step with him again.

Kurt wrapped his arm around her shoulders and brought her in close to his side. "You'll see."

Seconds later, they were in his pickup truck. At 10:00 p.m., the streets of Laramie were deserted. A few people had already put up their Christmas light displays. Paige took them in as Kurt drove the short distance to their neighborhood and turned into her driveway. Funny, she noted, how what had been her primary concern a week earlier was barely on her radar these days. "I wonder how far Rowdy and his crew have gotten on the plumbing," she murmured.

Kurt shrugged. "Only one way to find out."

Certain from the twinkle in his eyes that he knew something she didn't, Paige got out of the pickup. Together, they ambled up the walk toward the front door of her Queen Anne Victorian.

Seconds later, they walked through the portal and into the house.

Paige hit the light switch. Blinked twice, sure she couldn't possibly be seeing correctly. "It looks like it's finished!"

Kurt beamed and rocked back on his heels. "The paint and drywall subcontractors worked till midnight last night, but yep, it's all done and up and running. We can even test it, if you want."

Smiling with a mixture of pleasure and excitement, Paige strode past him to the kitchen at the rear of the house. It looked just as it had before the burst pipe and resulting flood. "Oh my…" she breathed. Turning on the kitchen faucet, she watched in amazement as a stream of water came pouring out. "I even have great water pressure now!"

Kurt smiled. "There's another surprise upstairs."

Aware how her pulse was jumping, her mind running riot with all sorts of sexy implications, Paige knitted her brows. "Like what?"

He refused to tell her anything else. "You'll have to go and see."

"Okay." She started off, but then became aware he wasn't following. "Aren't you coming?"

"Sure." He lazily caught up with her. Paige slipped her hand in his as they went up the stairs. Kurt squeezed her fingers affectionately and led her past the reading room and hall bath, to the bedroom next to the master suite.

Beside the guest bed was a full-size baby crib, complete with a musical mobile and frilly pink-and-white bedding and a rocking chair. "I had hoped to move you and the babies back here this evening," Kurt said softly.

For a second, Paige was so overcome she could barely speak.

Obviously misinterpreting her silence, he lifted a cautioning palm. "Which doesn't mean I'm not willing to keep helping out. I am. I just thought you'd be happier in your own place."

"You thought right," Paige said, pulling him toward her and gazing into his eyes. She welcomed the warmth and strength of his body pressed against hers.

She couldn't believe he had managed to meet her goal of being back in her own home by Thanksgiving Day! Especially after all the grief he'd given her on the matter, just one week ago. "But only on one condition," she teased mischievously.

"And that is?" Kurt countered, as if his only task was to keep her happy and make her his....

Paige wove her fingers around the nape of his neck and guided his mouth to hers. "You continue to stay with us."

Chapter Thirteen

Kurt hadn't expected Paige to kiss him. Up to now, he had been the one making all the moves. But he was very glad she did. The feel of her lips moving on his was more than just the ultimate turn-on; it made him feel more optimistic about the future than he'd been in a long time.

"Of course I'll stay with you and the babies." He wound his arms around her, brought her close. He threaded one hand through her hair and kissed her back, slowly and tenderly.

"Good." Paige took his hand and led him toward her bedroom, not stopping until they were next to her bed. "Because it wouldn't be the same without you."

Kurt knew it would have been better for the long haul if the two of them hadn't rushed into an affair, and instead had pursued the kind of slow, steady, getting-to-really-know-each-other phase vital to any strong, lasting relationship. But he couldn't turn away from her, not when she looked at him that way, so vulnerable, so full of yearning.

The truth was, he thought as he lowered his mouth to hers and used the gentle pressure of his lips to force hers apart, he needed to be close to her, too. Needed her to wrap her arms about his neck and press her breasts against his chest. Lower still, desire pooled. And she felt so good against him, so sweet and soft, feminine and sexy. Need surged inside him as their tongues tangled, searching, tasting, giving, taking. Kurt's body throbbed. He groaned and then let instinct and desire take over. He kissed her until he felt her body sway, and her surrender to him was inevitable.

He eased her out of the trim brown skirt and matching sweater she had worn to the festivities earlier in the day, then knelt to remove her suede heels. He hooked his hands in the waistband of her tights. She watched while he slowly peeled them down her long legs and drew them off. Admiring how she looked in the transparent chocolate-brown bra and bikini panties, he slipped his hands up and down her spine, across her shoulders, down her arms. Blood rushed to his groin as he reveled in the silkiness of her skin. Loving the way she arched against him, the way she trembled when they were about to make love, Kurt put everything he had into the kiss. He was determined this would be their most satisfying union yet, and that meant not letting her impatience as she reached for his belt, or the soft, helpless sounds she was making in the back of her throat, deter him.

"We'll both be naked," he told her, slipping the straps off her shoulders and baring her breasts, "soon enough."

"I don't know about that." She quivered as he stroked her nipples with the pads of his thumbs, took them in his mouth and laved them with his tongue. "Because I…

Ah, Kurt!" She caught his head in her hands, tangling her fingers in his hair.

He continued his slow exploration until she was breathless with sensation.

"Let me take my time loving you." He undid the clasp, then divested her of her bra.

"I don't think I can...." She moaned as he cupped her bottom, then hooked his hands in the elastic of her panties, dragging them down to the top of her thighs.

Kurt sat her down on the edge of the bed, planted a kiss in the auburn curls, and knowing exactly what she needed, drew her panties off the rest of the way. She moaned again as he kissed the inside of her thighs, her knees, then made his way slowly back up the length of her long sexy legs.

"This is torture," she breathed.

"The best kind," Kurt agreed. He throbbed with wanting her, with the need to let go, too, even as she surrendered to him completely. She was so incredibly beautiful, so responsive, so feminine. Reveling in the feel of her, he moved his thumb back and forth over her slick, sensitive center. Paige closed her eyes and let her head fall back. And still it wasn't enough for either of them. He loved her with his mouth, amazed at how ready she was for him, how welcoming. How her thighs fell farther open and her toes curled. She rocked against him, coming apart in his arms, letting him know without a doubt that she was his.

"I want you inside me," Paige gasped.

Needing to please her, to make her his, Kurt opened his trousers and shifted upward. She closed her hands around him and urged him closer. He covered her with his body and touched her with the tip of his manhood in the most intimate way.

"Yes," she whispered, her response honest and uncompromising. "I want you. Just like this. Now, Kurt..." she whimpered as he slid all the way home. "Yes."

Kurt kissed her again, hotter and harder this time. She took him farther into her, closing around him, giving him everything he had ever wanted, everything he had ever needed. Fire pooled in his groin as he went as deep as he could go, until sensation layered upon sensation, and what few boundaries remained between them dissolved. And they were as close as they could be.

Lips locked in a fierce, primal kiss, they catapulted into a serene satisfaction unlike anything Kurt had ever known.

KURT DRIFTED OFF TO SLEEP with Paige wrapped in his arms. He awakened several hours later to find her gone. He rubbed the sleep from his eyes and went off in search of her.

She had turned on the light and was standing next to the crib he had set up for the triplets. Wrapped in a robe, her auburn hair tousled, she looked beautiful and vulnerable, and to his surprise...almost sad. Which was, in his view, the last thing she should have been.

"Everything okay?" he asked, coming up behind her. Aware that he had never wanted a woman the way he wanted Paige, he wrapped his arms about her and buried his face in the fragrant softness of her hair.

She melted into the curve of his body. "Everything's fine."

Knowing her better than that by now, he challenged, "Then...?"

She turned to face him, the warm abundance of her breasts brushing his chest. "I woke up thinking I heard one of them cry, and came in here." Paige swallowed and pressed a knuckle to the corner of her eye. Releasing a breath, she continued, "It's silly, really. I mean, I knew they weren't here tonight, but instinct..." Her voice caught. She couldn't go on.

Kurt folded her close and ran his hands over her spine. "I miss them, too."

Paige bit her lip. Without warning, her eyes glistened with tears. "Kurt... What's going to happen if their mother changes her mind and wants them back?"

Refusing to consider anything less than a happy ending for all of them, he pushed the disturbing notion away. "I don't think that's going to happen." Certainly, from what he knew of human nature, the odds were against it....

"But if it does?"

Paige sounded so distraught he couldn't bear it. Kurt swallowed. "A decision will be made that is in the best interest of the babies," he told her gruffly. "Mitzy Martin and CPS will see to that. You know that."

Still looking as if she might burst into tears at any second, Paige gulped. "I do." She glanced back at the empty crib. "What time is it?"

Kurt checked his watch. "Four-fifteen."

"Do you think the triplets are up yet?"

"For my parents' sake," Kurt quipped, "hopefully not." He beckoned her with a sexy look and a tug of her hand. "Come back to bed." *So I can make love to you again.*

Still clearly missing the baby girls as much as he did, Paige dug in her heels, so Kurt promised, "We'll go over to the ranch as soon as our call ends, at seven. And then we'll hold Lindsay, Lori and Lucille and love 'em to our hearts' content."

Paige wrinkled her nose. "Wow…who knew you could be so sentimental?"

"Yeah, I know." He shook his head and made a perplexed face, then kissed the inside of her wrist. But he made no apologies. He'd grown incredibly attached to Paige and the girls over the past week. And he had no intention of giving them up. No matter how much a romantic fool he appeared to be….

"I just sounded like my mom there, didn't I?" he asked ruefully.

Paige laughed softly. "And mine. And every other hopelessly protective and adoring parent."

Which was, Kurt thought, exactly the way it should be.

They exchanged grins.

"Next you'll be sounding like your dad," Paige teased.

Kurt pressed a quick, affectionate kiss to her brow. "Then that makes two of us," he taunted, leading her back to bed for another round of lovemaking. "Because you're sounding an awful lot like a real parent, too."

PAIGE KNEW SOMETHING WAS up when she emerged from her bedroom, freshly showered and dressed, at seven in the morning. "What's going on?"

Kurt moved away from her computer, where he'd been checking his email via the web, before they left to pick up the kids. "I just had a message from a jewelry store in College Station."

The home of Texas A&M, where Kurt had gone to college.

"They sell the bracelet the babies are wearing in gold and sterling silver. Apparently, the filigree design is something particular to their store."

"Are they open yet?"

He regarded her in a way that left no doubt they would be making love again, very soon. "No. Not for another three hours. I already tried calling, and got nowhere. But I was able to send another email asking if they sold gold bracelets engraved with Lucille, Lindsay and Lori in the last year."

How easy it would be to depend on him this way, Paige thought. To feel there was no problem the two of them couldn't handle as long as they remained a team. She smiled. "You think they will tell us if they did?"

Kurt paused, his expression impatient. "Probably not without a search warrant, due to privacy issues for their customers. But I gave it a try. And if they do decline our request for information, we can always ask Kyle to follow up through the sheriff's department."

"Any further word from him?" Paige asked, aware that as nice as the night together had been, the real world was fast crowding in again.

Kurt shook his head. "No, but I've got my phone on." He reached over and squeezed her hand. "We're bound to hear something soon, from someone."

She nodded.

When the babies had first been left for Kurt on the McCabe doorstep, Paige had been hoping their mother, realizing her mistake, would reemerge to claim them.

Now her view was much more selfish, and she didn't know how she should feel about that. Happy that she had bonded so easily to babies she had not carried and given birth to herself? Or ashamed that she had it in her to put her own needs above everyone else's in this situation…?

"You okay?" Kurt asked, pulling her from her reverie.

Paige thrilled at the tender possessiveness in his voice. "I'm just…I miss the babies."

His mouth crooked again in that sexy grin. "Me, too," he confessed in a husky tone.

Thirty interminably long minutes later, they arrived at the McCabe ranch and found the babies had just been fed, diapered and changed. A thick quilt had been spread out over the family room carpet. All three infants were lying on their backs, kicking and waving their arms, happy as could be.

When they heard voices, they turned their heads toward Kurt and Paige.

"I think they know you're here," Annie noted, in that singsong tone adults used around babies.

The kicks and arm waving took on a more frantic pace.

Kurt slipped off his boots and sank down on the quilt next to them. Paige did the same.

Lucille cooed in response, Paige noted with affection and pride. Lindsay blinked her eyes repeatedly in a flirtatious manner and let out a gurgling sound. And

Lori seemed to be trying to flail her way into Kurt's arms as she blew little milk bubbles.

"I think Lucille is trying to talk to you," Paige said as the baby cooed even louder.

Kurt's brow furrowed. He turned and gave Paige the strangest look. "What about Lindsay?" he demanded.

Paige shrugged. "She's either got something in her eye or she's working on her flirting skills."

"And Lori?" Kurt pressed, even more curiously.

"Well, she's either practicing for the Olympics or trying to get up on her own," Paige said drolly.

Grinning widely, Kurt reached over and moved aside one ruffled pink sleeper sleeve to reveal a shiny gold bracelet, then another and another. "Well, I'll be..." he murmured, turning back to Paige, a mixture of admiration and wonder in his eyes. "You've just proved you can tell them apart now, just by looking."

Paige's jaw dropped; Kurt was right. She had just done that, without even thinking about it!

"Well, I'll be," she murmured softly.

Kurt grinned even wider and high-fived her. "Way to go, Mom!"

Paige was still reveling in that knowledge when the doorbell rang. Annie went to answer it, and moments later they heard the front door to the ranch house open and close.

Mitzy Martin was the first to appear. Then Kyle walked in, dressed in his khaki sheriff's department uniform, a beautiful dark-haired, thirtysomething woman beside him.

Kurt started in recognition as the woman turned her head away in embarrassment.

Obviously, Kurt and the dark-haired beauty were acquainted, Paige thought.

Realizing immediately, from the look on Mitzy's face and the expression on Kurt's, who she must be, Paige's heart sank.

They then advanced to the edge of the quilt, Mitzy flanking her on one side, Kyle on the other. Then he looked at the woman, every inch the lawman closing out a case. "Are these the children?" he asked quietly.

The beautiful woman nodded, her expression both careful and matter-of-fact.

Kyle stepped back from the blanket and turned to the adults. "Everyone, I'd like you to meet Tara Zimmerman."

But for Kurt, Paige noted unsteadily, no introduction was necessary. Which led her to wonder…what was his relationship with this woman? Was Kurt the babies' biological father, after all?

HIS EXPRESSION IMPLACABLE, Kurt stood, hands braced on his waist. "Tara and I met as college freshmen. She was my former organic chemistry lab partner at A&M."

Tara Zimmerman nodded, looking even more chagrined.

Annie's brow furrowed. "Did you two…?"

"No," Tara said quietly, as Mitzy stepped back to let the events unfold. "We never dated. But Kurt did regale me and everyone else with stories of growing up with a twin brother in a family that already boasted triplets. He made it sound like it had been so much fun, growing up a McCabe. And so…when I was looking for a solution to my dilemma regarding my own multiples, I thought of him. And did a little research, learned he was not yet married, but also knew he had always looked forward to having a family of his own one day...."

"Go on..." Kyle urged when she began to falter.

Tara took a deep breath, "When I was ready to let go, I brought the triplets here, and left them, knowing in my heart that if Kurt and the McCabes were involved, the girls would be very well taken care of. It eased my guilty conscience, knowing I was doing what was truly best for them."

For a moment the room was so silent they could have heard a pin drop.

Recognizing that Tara looked as if she might keel over from stress, Kurt moved to lace an arm about her waist. He led her over to the sofa to sit down, then hunkered beside her.

"What about their dad?" he asked quietly. "What does their father think about all this?"

"I had the babies via artificial insemination," Tara said, her cheeks flushing pink. "I did it to please the man I was dating. I wanted to marry him, but he refused because he thought I should have children, and he was sterile. I tried to convince him that having kids wasn't all that high on my priority list, but he didn't believe me." She took a deep breath and plunged on. "So I got the bright idea to go to a sperm bank and surprise him, thinking that if I were pregnant he would realize he could marry me after all, that he wouldn't be depriving me or himself of anything. Only instead of one baby, I ended up with three, and instead of wanting to marry me, he broke up with me and took off." Tara exhaled, obviously distraught.

"So there I was with three babies in my womb. And no husband or father for them." She shook her head, recalling her distress. "So I reached out to everyone I knew, all my former sorority sisters—that's where the ID bracelets came from…they were a gift from my old chapter. I also accepted a lot of help from my colleagues in the medical laboratory where I worked. I took money out of my retirement plan, so I could stay home for the first year. I hired a nurse to help me. And tried to make the best of it, but was completely and utterly miserable until I finally realized the truth." She paused to look everyone in the room in the eye. "I belong in a research lab, working to advance medical science! Not at home changing diapers."

Tara wrung her hands. "I tried telling people that I wasn't cut out for this and that I thought the babies would be better off with someone who really did want children." Her mouth twisted bitterly. "People looked at me like I was a heartless monster, or else crazy to give all this up. And I understand that. The babies are beautiful and smart and sweet. And I know they deserve so much more than I am ever going to be able to give them, feeling the way I do—not about them, but about motherhood in general."

Paige knew Tara was right. The worst thing she could do for the triplets was to let them grow up feeling like a burden. Or worse, technically cared for, but deep down, unwanted and unloved.

Tara lifted her hands in a helpless gesture. Her expression became all the more determined. "So I decided to forget about what people would think, and do what was best for the triplets. I brought them here, because I knew Kurt and I knew of the McCabes, and I felt confident that no matter what, the girls would be safe and taken care of. So…" Tara took a deep breath and turned her full attention back to Kurt. "If you're interested in being their father, Kurt, I want you to adopt them and bring them up as your own."

Paige's spirits rose. At last they were going to have the happy ending they had all been hoping for!

"Not so fast," Mitzy Martin said, stepping in.

Chapter Fourteen

The social worker looked at Tara Zimmerman. "Had you arranged to leave the babies with Kurt McCabe and his family before dropping them off here, or negotiated a private adoption from the outset, this situation would be quite different. However, you did not do that. Instead, you abandoned them and they became wards of the state. They were put into emergency foster care while Child Protective Services looked for you and a more permanent situation for them." She hesitated for a long moment. "After nearly seven days of searching, we've located a wonderful home for them in Laredo, Texas."

"Laredo!" Tara echoed, looking angry and confused.

"That's hours from here!" Paige noted, her own heart twisting with pain.

Kurt stepped forward, his body rigid. "I'd like them to stay here with us."

"That's what I want, too!" Tara cried. "Otherwise, I never would have left them with Kurt and the McCabes! I would have gone through regular channels to find another adoptive home."

"I wish you had," Mitzy remarked, not unkindly. "But you didn't. And now we have to deal with the situation in the time-honored way. And when we have multiples, our department policy is that we find one home for them, with a mother and a father who can accommodate the needs of multiple-birth children." Her tone turned crisp and professional. "As it happens, we have two wonderful, experienced foster parents who've been waiting for two years to foster-adopt. They are young and energetic. The woman is a former teacher who is now a stay-at-home mom. They've just seen the four children they were fostering be reunited with their parents. And they are ready, willing and able to take the triplets as soon as we clear it with the court Monday morning."

"What about us?" Kurt asked, his protective nature coming to the fore. "Don't Paige and I have a say in this?"

Mitzy sighed. "I can't thank you enough for what you and Paige have done for these kids. You've put your lives on hold to take care of them. And you've done an amazing job. But the two of you aren't married. And although Paige has been planning to have a child for some time now, outside the boundaries of marriage…" Mitzy paused and looked long and hard at Kurt. "You've never shown the least bit of interest in settling down and having kids. In fact, if memory serves, when you had a chance to get engaged to Camila Albright, you broke up with her."

Kurt grimaced. "Actually, Camila broke up with me."

Mitzy waved her hand. "Whatever. The point is, Kurt, these kids need a stable, loving home, and they need it now. As the social worker in charge of their case, it's my job to do what is best for them, and I'm going to recommend they be placed with the family in Laredo. In the meantime, I would like to leave the babies with you and Paige for the weekend, so you'll have time to say goodbye." She turned to the triplets' mother. "Tara, I'd like you to come with me and Kyle. We have a lot to go over and some paperwork to fill out. And if you wouldn't mind, we'd like you to speak with our staff psychologist, just to make sure this is the right decision before you sever all ties with the children."

Tara nodded and, appearing a little dazed, left with the social worker and the lawman.

Kurt's parents looked as devastated as Paige felt.

Kurt faced Annie and Travis McCabe. "Mom, Dad, would you mind watching the kids while Paige and I stepped outside to talk for a bit?"

Annie gazed at them with gentle compassion. "Not at all. Go ahead, and take your time. The girls will be fine."

Numbly, Paige followed Kurt into the foyer, let him help her on with her jacket, and then watched as he slipped on his. Together, they stepped out onto the porch where the babies had been found. Her shoulders slumping, she followed him the length of the wrap-around porch, to the side of the rambling, one-story ranch house. Travis perched on the wooden railing, his long legs stretched out, his hands braced on either side of him. She thrust her hands in the pockets of her jacket and leaned against the stone.

"We have to fight this," he stated.

Paige wished that were possible. The commonsense

side of her knew it would be a wasted effort. "How?" she echoed, surprised by the listless sound of her voice echoing in the chilly afternoon air. The sky above was as gray and gloomy as her mood. "We're not married."

Kurt shrugged. "We could be."

She blinked, certain she hadn't heard correctly.

"Seriously," he continued urgently, "if that's what it takes…"

Paige's jaw dropped. "You're asking me to marry you so we can adopt the babies?" It sounded even more ludicrous when she said it.

Kurt's eyes remained on hers. "If that's the only way we can compete with this other couple." He was ready to do whatever it took.

Hurt mingled with the shock deep inside her. "I thought we were past that."

He regarded her stoically. "What?"

"Competing!" She threw up her palms and pushed away from the wall, moving closer. "The whole rivalry business!"

He shot up from the rail and approached her. "This isn't a game, Paige."

Tears pushed at her eyes, but she refused to let them fall. "I know that!" she cried, wishing they could afford to be selfish here, knowing they could not. "Do you?"

He glared down at her, clearly affronted by her uncooperative attitude. "I love those little girls," he said hoarsely.

She knew that. "So do I!" Paige countered emotionally. It was Kurt's lack of love for her that was the problem here. Why couldn't he see that?

He gestured with an impatient hand. "Their mother wants me and my family to bring them up."

Pain swelled in Paige's chest. "You and your family being the operative points." She forced herself to say the words that were lodged in her throat. "I'm not in this equation, Kurt."

"You would be if Tara had seen you with them this last week and realized what an integral part to this situation you are. You're an incredibly loving, giving mother."

"Who wants a child of her own to love and care for," Paige interjected softly. *Now more than ever.*

The lines around his mouth tightened. "We're talking about your plans to be artificially inseminated tomorrow?"

"Yes."

His expression was stark. "You'd do that…*now*…with all we have on the line?"

What choice did she have if she still wanted a family? And she did. "I told you, Kurt. The girls' fate is out of our hands."

"Not if we fight with all our might to keep them!"

"Listen to me, Kurt. The triplets deserve more than two parents who've come together only to care for them. They need a family with a solid foundation, and that requires the kind of deep, everlasting love both our sets of parents have for each other."

Hurt flickered briefly on his face, before morphing into a disappointment that seemed to go soul-deep. "So you won't help me?"

"The girls need a mother and a father who love each other, as well as them."

A muscle ticked in Kurt's jaw. "They need stability!"

"Exactly! You and I have been able to get along with each other for only one week!"

"Because we didn't really know each other back then. Now we do."

"Then you must realize that I won't..." Paige paused and dug her fingernails into her palms. "I *can't* be selfish in this situation." *It doesn't matter how much I've enjoyed being your friend and lover, or how close I sometimes thought you might be to falling in love with me.*

Paige knew she had to deal with the reality of the situation, not what she wished it was, or one day would be.

And the bottom line was Kurt did not love her. Not the way she needed and wanted to be loved to make their relationship work long-term.

"You're the least selfish person I know," he interjected.

"Then let me do the right thing." Her voice broke. "The girls deserve the kind of stable, loving, dependable family we both grew up with."

"You and I can give them that."

No, Paige thought sadly, they couldn't. Not without a foundation of enduring love. Like it or not, she had to bail out now, while they still had a chance to do it with the least amount of collateral damage. A single tear slipped out of her eye and down her cheek. "I have to do what's right," she repeated thickly as more tears followed.

"So do I," Kurt said grimly, the look in his eyes

saying he would never ever forgive her for this. "Even if it's without your help!"

"I DON'T UNDERSTAND," Annie McCabe said, several minutes later. She looked out the window to see Paige wheeling her own suitcase to the car. "Paige is leaving?"

"We decided it would be best if we split up the parenting duty and I cared for the triplets here today and tomorrow during the day." *While she has her appointment at the fertility clinic.*

Kurt swallowed back the hurt and resentment growing inside him. He had offered Paige more than he had ever offered any woman in his entire life, and what had she done? She'd told him, "No, thanks." And all because what they had forged this last week didn't live up to some idea of perfection that she thought both their parents' marriages had.

Instead of doing what was needed—when it was needed—she had let him know what he offered her wasn't good enough, and she'd walked away. From him and the kids!

Aware that his mother was waiting to hear the rest of their plans, Kurt pushed aside his humiliation and said, "Then we'll do the switch at her home in town, tomorrow evening. That way we'll have equal time with the girls, and Paige will be able to say her goodbyes to them in private."

"She's not going to help you fight to keep them here?"

Silence stretched between him. His mother seemed to know she had struck a nerve, and simply waited.

Knowing she would get the information out of him one way or another, Kurt met her eyes and said contemptuously, "Paige doesn't feel it's in the babies' best interest to be brought up by the two of us."

Her expression perplexed, Annie kept her eyes firmly locked with his. "Okay. What am I missing?" she said finally in that soft, tender voice that always tore him up inside. "Because yesterday, at the Thanksgiving dinner, you all were one big happy family. And I could have sworn by the way you were both acting that you wanted to adopt these babies together."

Kurt blew out a weary breath. He didn't want to be rude, but he didn't want to discuss this like some brokenhearted fool, either, even if that was exactly what he was! "That was before Mitzy weighed in and put the guilt trip on us because we're not married and this other couple is. But that could be easily remedied!"

"Tell me you did not propose marriage to Paige that way," Annie said gently.

"She's a practical woman. Idealistic to the extreme. Of course she is going to want to be married in that situation."

"For love—not convenience. Oh my goodness!" His mom threw up her hands in frustration. "Haven't I taught my sons anything?"

"Well, obviously, yes. Since three of my brothers are married with children."

Annie blew out a frustrated breath. "Apparently, I let the lessons slide when it came to you and Kyle, because neither of you is showing the least bit of interest in really settling down. Until yesterday, anyway, and then I could have sworn…" She stopped and studied him shrewdly.

"You love her, don't you? That's why you're so upset! It isn't just the babies, although that's a big part of it. It's the fact that Paige turned you down."

Figuring he'd endured enough indignity for one day, Kurt folded his arms across his chest. "Are we finished?" He pushed the words through clenched teeth.

His mother caught his arm, forcing him to face her. "As soon as I say one more thing. You love those babies enough to go after custody of them. If you love Paige, you'll go after her the same way."

"Dad, can you ask Mom if she knows where I put the baby shampoo?" Paige said early Sunday evening as she was getting ready to give the kids their baths for the very last time. Her mother and father had come over to help.

"Will do." Her dad disappeared, Lindsay in his arms.

He returned moments later, still holding the baby. Her mom was right beside him, cuddling Lucille. Dani regard Paige with a quiet, assessing look while Paige gently worked the soft cotton sleeper from Lori. "I just talked to Annie McCabe on the phone. Kurt is fighting to keep the kids with everything he has." Dani edged closer. "Are you sure you don't want to join him?"

Paige lowered Lori into the baby bathtub. She put a washcloth over the infant's chest to help keep her warm.

In a perfect world, of course she would join Kurt! In a perfect world, he would have said he loved her before asking her to marry him. Wishing she wasn't so vulnerable where he was concerned, she sighed. "Believe me, Mom, I've done nothing but think about it for the last two days." She'd thought about it when she went to the hospital to check on her patients, when she tried to pick the right daddy for the baby she wanted to have, and when she arrived at the fertility clinic. And she'd thought about it all day long as she cared for the triplets this one last time....

Sadly, Paige confided, "As much as we love them, we can't give them what they need."

"A two-parent home," Dani guessed.

Paige gently lathered shampoo into Lori's dark curls. "Right."

Dani reached over to help rinse the soap from Lori's tiny body.

"Nor can you fulfill all their basic needs," Beau guessed, as he held out a towel.

Paige's spine stiffened defensively as she picked up Lori and handed her to her father to hold. "Well, that we can do," she said indignantly. "We already have, for days now!"

Dani exchanged looks with her husband, then finished undressing Lucille and handed her to Paige. "They also need love...."

Paige eased Lucille into the baby bath, smiling as the little girl gurgled in delight. Working to conceal her aggravation—she certainly didn't want to upset the babies—she told her mother in the most even voice she could manage, "We love them."

"They need attention, too." Her father frowned as he realized he had messed up the snaps on Lori's pink-and-white sleep suit.

Paige did her best not to harrumph. "We certainly

paid them tons of attention and would continue to do so if we adopted them." That wasn't the point!

Dani shampooed Lucille's halo of dark curls and gently soaped her body. "They would also need baby-sitters or a nanny or two when you both went back to work."

This time Paige rinsed, and held out the towel. "We could supply that."

Beau set Lori down where she could watch the goings-on, then began diapering Lucille. "They'd also need extended family to love them," he said.

Paige rolled her eyes as her mother slid Lindsay into the waiting bath. "You know they'd get that, from both sides of the family!" she snapped, irritated by the good cop, bad cop routine her parents always employed when they thought she was on the wrong path.

Dani allowed Paige to take over. "Then what's missing?" she queried, watching as Paige soaped, rinsed and wrapped Lindsay in a towel, too. "Except marriage."

Heart aching at the memory of that debacle, Paige handed Lindsay over for her father to dress.

"Wait," Dani said, emptying out the baby bathtub into the sink. She paused to snap her fingers, as if suddenly recalling something. "Kurt proposed!"

Paige flushed. *Guilty as charged.* "Who told you that?" she demanded.

Her mother's eyes radiated sympathy. "Annie McCabe deduced as much from what Kurt didn't say."

Together, Paige and her parents picked up the babies and headed downstairs to the kitchen, where three bottles of formula were waiting to be heated. "It wasn't much of a proposal." Paige hit the buttons on the warmers, one after another.

Beau shook his head in silent chastisement, even as he rocked Lindsay back and forth in his strong arms. "And it certainly didn't come from his heart," he surmised.

"Well, now, I wouldn't go so far as to say that!" Paige stated. "I'm sure Kurt was sincere when he proposed. The problem was he asked me to be his wife for all the wrong reasons!"

Beau frowned. "Those being?"

"He didn't ask because we had some grand love." At least not on his side of the equation, Paige added sadly to herself. On her side, she had to admit, the love was there. "He asked because he had really come to love the kids and he knew I had, too. And it was the practical thing to do."

Dani accepted the warmed bottle Paige handed her, and offered it to the babe in her arms. "That still seems strange. As long as I've known Kurt—or maybe I should say during the many, *many* years he has been a burr under your saddle—he never once struck me as the kind of guy who would automatically do what was expected of him, even to attain a goal."

Paige's spine stiffened. "He doesn't."

Beau smiled as he gave Lindsay her bottle. "So why would he suddenly ask you to marry him just because it's what someone else expects?"

"Because he's a very realistic person." *Not an idealist like me.* "And he thinks that's the only way he'll be able to convince the court that he has more to offer the kids than the couple in Laredo."

"Kurt's attorney doesn't seem to think so," Beau

interjected bluntly. "He thinks it's entirely possible Kurt will be able to convince the judge without him being married, as long as he has all his ducks in a row. And he's spent the entire weekend doing just that."

Shock warred with hope. "He's really going to do this, all on his own?"

Dani nodded. "He really is. Our question to you is—are you going to be part of the support system lining up to take care of these kids? Or will you be standing on the sidelines, waiting for everything to align perfectly before you act?"

Her emotions in turmoil, Paige thought all night about what her parents had said, and she was still thinking about it the next morning as she got the triplets ready to go to court. "Saying goodbye is going to be hard," she told Lucille, Lindsay and Lori, trying not to cry as she fastened them into their car seats one by one. It was difficult to be noble, when all she wanted to do was follow her heart. "But we'll all be okay. Seriously."

Her spirits sank even lower when they all began to pout.

Paige swallowed. "Please don't look at me like I'm letting you down." She blinked back the welling tears. "I'm making sure that you go to a good home."

Lucille gurgled, as if to disagree.

"I know Kurt provided that, too," Paige soothed.

Lori kicked.

"But that was when we were both taking care of you together," Paige continued calmly as Lindsay waved her tiny fist in the air. "That wasn't a realistic predictor of the future."

All three babies quieted and just stared at her.

"I'm doing what is best for all of us in letting you go," she said with as much tranquility as she could muster. But if that was the case…why didn't she believe it?

PAIGE EXPECTED KURT WOULD have a support system with him when she arrived at the Laramie County Courthouse, but she hadn't counted on Tara Zimmerman, his attorney *and* an entire McCabe army. His parents, his brothers and their wives, plus most of his aunts and uncles—even his grandparents, John and Lilah McCabe—were all there, ready to do battle with him.

Everyone, it seemed, but her.

Drawing a deep breath, she pushed the buggy toward him.

Mitzy Martin came toward her, from the left. "Thanks for bringing the triplets," she told her. Clearly, the social worker was ready to take over. The only problem was, Paige wasn't any more willing to let go of the babies now than she was ready to let go of all she and Kurt had found together during the last week.

He looked incredibly pulled together in a dark suit and tie. There was no clue what he was thinking or feeling until he gazed down at the babies with unstinting tenderness and affection. Lindsay, Lori and Lucille were cuddled together as if they knew something was up.

Hoping and praying it wasn't too late to rectify the biggest mistake she had ever made in her life, Paige reluctantly let Mitzy take charge of the triplets, then looked at Kurt. "May I have a word with you?"

His attorney stepped in. "I don't think it's wise."

Paige ignored him. "Please," she said to Kurt. "It's important."

He nodded.

"Five minutes, that's it," the attorney stipulated. "You can't afford to be late."

Kurt indicated he understood, then waved everyone toward the courtroom. "You all go ahead. I have something I want to say to Paige, too."

Whether that was good or bad was impossible to tell.

Kurt turned and walked down the hall. Her heart pounding, Paige followed him outside to the limestone courthouse steps. It was a beautiful November day, sunny and clear, the temperature hovering around sixty.

He turned to face her. He had never looked sexier. Nor more unapproachable. There was so much to say that she didn't know where to begin. Fortunately, Kurt did it for her. "How did your appointment go on Saturday?" he asked, his voice laced with unexpected tenderness and concern.

"I didn't go." Her own voice dropped a notch.

Abruptly, he grew very still. "Why not?"

Unable to help herself, Paige moved a step closer, so they were standing just inches apart. She knew it was time to bare her soul to him. She slipped her hand in his and held tight. "I realized that's not the way I want to have a baby. Especially when there are three little girls in my life I would still very much like to mother." She blinked back the mist of emotion, finally daring to put it all on the line. "Oh, Kurt, I'm so sorry. I should have stood by you. I should have helped you fight to keep the babies."

His gaze remained on hers, as strong and steady as his presence. "Why didn't you?" he asked softly.

Paige's heart began to pound. Hope rose within her. "I was afraid I wasn't going to be enough. Not for them, not for you. I thought they deserved perfection."

He tightened his grip on her hand and tugged her close. "And now?" He wrapped his arm about her waist and held fast.

Paige splayed her hands across his chest. She couldn't help but notice how strong and warm and solid Kurt felt. Or how good he smelled, like soap and cologne. Everything about them felt so right. "I realize perfection is overrated. What the triplets really need—" she paused to look deep into his eyes "—what we all need is love. And I have so much of that to give."

He tilted his head, studying her, as if wanting to believe. "Familial love?"

"Yes."

Here was the risk, and it was a big one, but she was ready.

Paige drew a bolstering breath. "And another kind of love, too," she said courageously, winding her arms about his neck. "The kind a woman feels for her man. The kind I have for you...the kind that will last forever."

Kurt grinned. Threading his hands through her hair, he gave her the kind of kiss she had been waiting for her whole life, the kind that promised a lifetime of love and affection, trust and understanding.

"I have that kind of love for you, too," he murmured finally. "And I have something else." His expression as tender as his voice, Kurt took a narrow, blue velvet box from his inside jacket pocket. "The girls and I planned to give it to you later, after we'd succeeded in court, but maybe now is the perfect time, after all."

Her fingers shaking as much as the rest of her, Paige opened the lid. Inside were two filigreed gold ID bracelets, identical to the ones the triplets were wearing. One was inscribed Daddy, the other Mommy.

Paige's eyes blurred as Kurt took the one engraved for her, and put it on her wrist. He fastened the clasp, then drew back to look at her, his smile radiating hope and happiness. "I didn't give up on you, either," he said, all the commitment she'd ever wanted reflected in his deep blue eyes. "Say you'll marry me, Paige."

With joy filling her heart, Paige whispered back, "You better believe I will."

Epilogue

Nearly five years later...

"Are the new babies going to be boys or girls?" Lucille asked Paige and Kurt, with her typical "need to know," as the five of them gathered in the kitchen.

Looking more beautiful than ever to Kurt, Paige smiled, her hand automatically going to her slightly swollen tummy. "Three boys."

"That means we're going to have *brothers,*" Lindsay announced seriously, her dark curls bobbing.

"Only they won't be as old as us or as big as us," Lori added importantly, her blue eyes widening, "because we're five years old today. Aren't we, Daddy?"

Kurt nodded affectionately. "Yes, you are," he told their three daughters.

And what a great five years it had been, Kurt thought contentedly. He and Paige had decided to take their time before saying "I do," because he had wanted her to have the courtship she deserved. They had married the week before the triplets' first birthday, in an outdoor arbor on Paige's parents' ranch, with all their friends and family as witnesses. The days before the nuptials and ever since had been filled to the brim. He'd loved every action-packed moment of their life together, and so had Paige. And now they were expecting again, this time the old-fashioned way, as well as preparing for yet another big family party.

"Okay, ladies." Paige helped the girls into their appropriately sized aprons. "What color frosting are we going to have on this cake?"

"Pink!" all three yelled in unison.

"What happened to lavender?" Kurt teased, pretending to be terribly confused by their decision.

"Daddy, that was last week's favorite color!" Lucille said.

"We can't have the same color two weeks in a row!" Lindsay leaned over to watch Paige shake two drops of red food coloring into the buttercream.

"So this week it's pink!" Lori explained.

Paige grinned. Color was one of the few things their three little girls agreed upon. In every other way, they were completely unique, which was the way she and Kurt wanted it. "Then pink it is," she decreed, dividing the frosting equally into three bowls.

Kurt brought over the vanilla sheet cake and centered it on the counter in front of them. "What are you all wearing to the party?"

"My pink ballerina outfit!" Lindsay heaped a big glob of icing on her share of the cake and spread it around with a child-size plastic spatula.

"My pink cowgirl hat and boots, and my pink jeans and sparkly pink T-shirt," Lucille said, spreading frosting carefully around the edges of the section she was decorating.

"I'm wearing my pink princess dress and my pink polka-dot slippers." Lori delicately dotted the cake with icing.

Kurt used his index finger to scoop a little leftover icing from the stainless steel mixing bowl and turned to offer the rest to Paige. "What are you wearing, *Mommy?*"

Paige smiled at the soft endearment in her husband's voice, and all that one word had come to mean, as she brought out the candies they would use to decorate the icing.

There was no doubt their lives had changed for the better when they had all come together. The girls had the love and family they needed, as did she and Kurt. The foundation for all that happiness was the strong, passionate, accepting union she and Kurt had forged.

Through each other, they both had changed.

She was able to live in the moment more.

He planned further ahead.

They both knew they didn't have to be perfect, but they did have to commit to be there for each other for the rest of their lives.

And that, they found, was very easy to do when two people loved each other as much as they did....

"Are you going to wear your pink shoes or the yellow ones?" Lucille pressed.

Her flats sounded oh-so-comfortable. "The pink ones, I think." Paige scooped up a little icing, too. She savored the sweet taste on her tongue. "And my pink sundress and matching summer cardigan."

The girls exchanged glances, communicating without

saying a word. "Can Daddy wear pink, too?" Lucille asked finally.

Lindsay suggested helpfully, "We want to get him a pink shirt!"

"That way he can match us!" Lori explained.

Paige turned to Kurt.

Although her dear husband was blessedly poker-faced, she knew him well enough to realize all he wasn't saying. "Pink is not really Daddy's color," she told the girls.

Kurt grinned at her and winked. "I'd take one for the team."

"I know you would." She patted him on the chest, above his oh-so-generous heart. But she also knew that his brothers would never let him live it down. She regarded their daughters. "What do you say we all dress alike in some other way?"

The girls thought. Then smiled, as recognition hit.

"I know!" Lucille cried in glee.

"We can all wear our bracelets!" Lori declared.

"And that way we'll all match! Same as always!" Lindsay said.

"Good idea," Paige stated.

So that was exactly what they did.

And six months later, when the three little brothers came along, they received ID bracelets, too, from their mommy and daddy and three big sisters. So that, as their sisters lovingly explained, they could all "match" and be part of their big happy family. And—as an added bonus—be identified correctly....

After the girls left the hospital to go home with their grandparents, and their three brothers were whisked back to the nursery, Paige and Kurt were alone together once again.

"Now that you've gifted me with sons," he said, pulling another little blue velvet box from his pocket, "I have a present for you."

Thrilling at her husband's tender generosity, Paige opened it.

Inside was a gold necklace with three charms in the center: a key, a lock and a heart.

She looked up at Kurt, not sure she understood. "That," he told her hoarsely, "is for you. Because you had the key to unlock my heart."

The tears of joy she'd been holding back slid down her face.

"I love you, Paige," Kurt whispered, taking her in his arms and kissing her sweetly.

"Oh, Kurt," she murmured, stroking his stubble-roughened cheek and leaning toward him. She knew as many times as she told him, she would never say it enough. "I love you, too, so much." She kissed him back and held him close. "You really have made all my dreams come true."

* * * * *

Welcome back, McCabes!
Watch for Cathy Gillen Thacker's new miniseries
TEXAS LEGACIES: THE McCABES
starting with
A COWBOY UNDER
THE MISTLETOE.
Only from Harlequin American Romance!

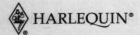

HARLEQUIN®

COMING NEXT MONTH

Available November 9, 2010

#1329 THE SHERIFF'S CHRISTMAS SURPRISE
Babies & Bachelors USA
Marie Ferrarella

#1330 JESSE: MERRY CHRISTMAS, COWBOY
The Codys: The First Family of Rodeo
Lynnette Kent

#1331 SANTA IN A STETSON
Fatherhood
Rebecca Winters

#1332 MIRACLE BABY
Baby To Be
Laura Bradford

REQUEST YOUR FREE BOOKS!

2 FREE NOVELS PLUS 2 FREE GIFTS!

HARLEQUIN®

American ★ Romance®

Love, Home & Happiness!

YES! Please send me 2 FREE Harlequin® American Romance® novels and my 2 FREE gifts (gifts are worth about $10). After receiving them, if I don't wish to receive any more books, I can return the shipping statement marked "cancel." If I don't cancel, I will receive 4 brand-new novels every month and be billed just $4.24 per book in the U.S. or $4.99 per book in Canada. That's a saving of at least 15% off the cover price! It's quite a bargain! Shipping and handling is just 50¢ per book.* I understand that accepting the 2 free books and gifts places me under no obligation to buy anything. I can always return a shipment and cancel at any time. Even if I never buy another book from Harlequin, the two free books and gifts are mine to keep forever.

154/354 HDN E5LG

Name _____ (PLEASE PRINT)

Address _____ Apt. #

City _____ State/Prov. _____ Zip/Postal Code

Signature (if under 18, a parent or guardian must sign)

Mail to the **Harlequin Reader Service:**
IN U.S.A.: P.O. Box 1867, Buffalo, NY 14240-1867
IN CANADA: P.O. Box 609, Fort Erie, Ontario L2A 5X3

Not valid for current subscribers to Harlequin® American Romance® books.

Want to try two free books from another line?
Call 1-800-873-8635 or visit www.morefreebooks.com.

* Terms and prices subject to change without notice. Prices do not include applicable taxes. N.Y. residents add applicable sales tax. Canadian residents will be charged applicable provincial taxes and GST. Offer not valid in Quebec. This offer is limited to one order per household. All orders subject to approval. Credit or debit balances in a customer's account(s) may be offset by any other outstanding balance owed by or to the customer. Please allow 4 to 6 weeks for delivery. Offer available while quantities last.

Your Privacy: Harlequin is committed to protecting your privacy. Our Privacy Policy is available online at www.eHarlequin.com or upon request from the Reader Service. From time to time we make our lists of customers available to reputable third parties who may have a product or service of interest to you. If you would prefer we not share your name and address, please check here. ☐

Help us get it right—We strive for accurate, respectful and relevant communications. To clarify or modify your communication preferences, visit us at www.ReaderService.com/consumerchoice.

HAR10R

*See below for a sneak peek from
our inspirational line, Love Inspired® Suspense*

*Enjoy this heart-stopping excerpt from
RUNNING BLIND
by top author Shirlee McCoy,
available November 2010!*

**The mission trip to Mexico was supposed to be an
adventure. But the thrill turns sour when Jenna Dougherty
and her roommate Magdalena are kidnapped.**

"It's okay. I'm here to help." The voice was as deep as the
darkness, but Jenna Dougherty didn't believe the lie. She
could do nothing but lie still as hands slid down her arms,
felt the rope around her wrists.

"I'm going to use a knife to cut you free, Jenna. Hold
still."

The cold blade of a knife pressed close to her head before
her gag fell away.

"I—" she started, but her mouth was dry, and she could
do nothing but suck in air.

"Shhh. Whatever needs to be said can be said when
we're out of here." Nick spoke quietly, his hand gentle on
her cheek. There and gone as he sliced through the ropes on
her wrists and ankles.

He pulled her upright. "Come on. We may be on
borrowed time."

"I can't leave my friend," Jenna rasped out.

"There's no one here. Just us."

"She has to be here." Jenna took a step away.

"There's no one here. Let's go before that changes."

"It's dark. Maybe if we find a light…"

"What did you say?"

"We need to turn on the light. I can't leave until I know that—"

"What can you see, Jenna?"

"Nothing."

"No shadows? No light?"

"No."

"It's broad daylight. There's light spilling in from the window I climbed in through. You can't see it?"

She went cold at his words.

"I can't see anything."

"You've got a nasty bruise on your forehead. Maybe that has something to do with it." His fingers traced the tender flesh on her forehead.

"It doesn't matter *how* it happened. I'm blind!"

Can Nick help Jenna find her friend or will chasing this trail have Jenna running blindly again into danger?

Find out in RUNNING BLIND, available in November 2010 only from Love Inspired Suspense.